WAYWARD SKY

SOULS OF THE ROAD -3

DEVON MONK

ODD
HOUSE
PRESS

Wayward Sky

Copyright © 2022 by Devon Monk

ISBN: 9781939853318

Publisher: Odd House Press

Cover Art: Ravven

Interior Design: Odd House Press

To my family - and all the dreamers on the road

ACKNOWLEDGMENTS

I would like to give my deepest gratitude to the people who contributed to this book and helped me make it so much better.

Thank you Ravven, for your wonderful artwork. I love the strong, but dreamy, dust-and-denim mood you bring to these covers. It's so perfectly Route 66.

Thank you to my incredibly patient copy editor, Sharon Elaine Thompson, for helping to make this shine, even if your broken wrist meant for a much quicker pass. I've done my best to pick up where you left off.

Readers, if there are errors in this book, they are wholly mine alone.

Huge thank you to my best friend and beta reader, Dejsha Knight for reading this on such short notice and letting me know the good parts, the rough parts, and that the ending needed a little tweak. As always, my dearest, you are a treasure.

Thank you Deadline Dames Rachel Vincent and Rinda Elliott, for meeting us on the Route at Pops. It was great to catch up with you, and to experience the soda ranch in person. I put it in the book!

To my husband Russ, and my sons Kameron and

Konner, I love you. Thank you for sharing your lives with me. You are the very best part of mine.

And to my readers: thank you for traveling with Lula and Brogan one more time down this magical road. Until next time, safe travels, and happy reading!

CHAPTER ONE

The only good thing about being a spirit cursed to haunt Route 66, was that at least as a spirit, I hadn't had to worry about trying to sleep in the back of Silver, the old truck my wife, Lula had insisted on buying a couple months ago.

I hadn't had to worry about being in a field in the middle of nowhere Kansas, with metal edges digging into my ass every time I turned over, either.

I exhaled and shifted, shoehorning myself between the wheel wells, claiming a sliver of mattress crowded with five other bodies sprawled around me.

Sure, it'd been lonely following Lula as she traveled the Mother Road for nearly a hundred years, hunting for the monsters who had attacked us, leaving her a *thrawn*, which was one step away from becoming a vampire, and me a tethered spirit.

But if there had been one small good—maybe infinitesimal, but still good—benefit to being a spirit, it was that I'd had a little room to move.

I rolled my foot, trying to ease the promise of a cramp in my calf.

"Okay?" Lula asked softly, as I shifted my hip yet again.

"Motels have soft beds," I said into her hair, stretching my toes.

"You hate motels," she replied. "They have ghosts, which you also hate."

"True." I couldn't remember the last time I'd won this conversation. Every time she checked into a place for the night, she'd worry I'd have to deal with hostile souls, so she avoided motels. It was partly why she'd bought this truck. It had sleeping space for two.

Two. We hadn't planned on picking up people along the way.

"But *you* like motels," I said, giving it the old college try.

"I like the truck. I like the open sky and the stars."

Moonlight filtered down through the oak trees around us. We'd parked the truck in a field, far enough from the road we wouldn't be bothered.

She repositioned in my arms, pressed her back more firmly to my chest and pulled my arms closer around her. She closed her hand over mine, which rested against her stomach, and looked over her shoulder. "I like being here, in your arms."

The look in her eyes was a story of its own. She'd missed the flesh of me, the realness of me. Nearly a hundred years without being in each other's arms was a lot to make up for. We'd held on for this chance, for someday having each other again.

Having this again.

"Still," I said, "it's pretty crowded."

She snuggled closer. "I like it fine. I've slept alone for enough years. This is good."

She was not wrong.

My shoulder under her head was falling asleep, the cramp in my leg bit harder no matter how I stretched my foot, and my back hurt.

But when Lula said she wanted nothing more than to lie in my arms, there was no possibility I'd say otherwise.

Abbi—who currently looked like a stout ten-year-old girl, but who was actually the rabbit who lived in the moon—started the night sleeping beside Lula. But she'd wriggled and squirmed, tossed and huffed until she'd ended up sprawled above both our heads, stretched out and dreaming.

Abbi had been excited about the camp out. She might act like the shaggy white-haired girl she appeared to be, but she'd come down from the moon searching for her lost shadow and protector, who had been stolen by the foul Hush creatures who lived beneath the hills of Missouri. We'd found her living with a pack of were-wolves who adored her.

We'd saved her shadow, Hado, and saved her, too. Then she'd surprised us by choosing to travel with Lula and me.

Said it felt right.

Said she always wanted a family.

I'd always wanted a family too, but that hope had

been buried in grave dirt the day Lula and I had been attacked by monsters and cursed to follow Route 66.

Lu pressed back into me more and a bolt dug into my hip, bruising. Abbi smacked her lips and flipped onto one side, her stockinged feet flopping into my face.

I winced and let out a sigh. "You are a full-grown moon deity," I hissed, plucking her ankle off my forehead. "Keep your big feet to yourself."

Hado, who preferred the form of a black panther but had wisely chosen to shift into the shape of a small black cat tonight, lifted his head. His luminous gray eyes scanned for threats and stopped on me.

He stared, gaze focused on my hand on Abbi's foot.

He did not approve of me manhandling the Moon Rabbit.

I gently pushed Abbi's feet up off my face without looking away from Hado. Abbi snorted and flipped the other way, pulling the rest of my pillow up into her arms. Half a breath later, she snored. Loudly.

"Aces," I grumbled as mosquitos buzzed around my ear, immune to the chemical spray Lula had drenched me in hours ago.

"She's fine," I loud-whispered to Hado. I slapped my cheek, the wet smear of bug guts adding to the evening's delights. "She's sleeping better than any of us, the little traitor."

The feline creature blinked, and I had the distinct feeling he was laughing at me.

Swell. Just keen.

He lowered his head and curled back up against

Lorde, our big fluffy black chow chow-shepherd mix who was taking up all the remaining space at our feet.

Lorde slept so peacefully, I thought maybe I oughta crawl down there with her, even though there was no room for my legs to stretch out. At least maybe Lorde and Hado wouldn't steal my pillow.

A bug landed on my ear and bit hard.

I grunted and slapped it.

Twice.

Three for good measure.

Lu's breathing didn't change, but there was a sense of awareness in her silence that was unmistakable.

"Sleep," I said, just that little bit louder, flicking crushed wings and shell off my neck. "I'm fine."

A heel hit the top of my head, twisted, and then the rest of the foot settled there like a cap.

"For fuck of all." I—gently—removed her foot, and then sat.

The air was humid, heavy and warm, although the hint of a breeze promised relief. But this was late summer in east Kansas. Any rest from the heat would be temporary.

Lu turned to lie on her back, her braided hair a dusky flame against her astonishingly pale skin. Those honey eyes watched me, and all the world slipped away.

"Do you want to switch sides?" She turned her hand, palm up, and as I always had, as I always would, I dropped my hand to hers.

The warmth of her skin, like heated silk against mine, was still a wonder. I'd only been back in living flesh for two months now, and the sensations of living were still new.

"No. It's fine," I said. "Go back to sleep. I just need to stretch my legs."

She squeezed my hand. "I'll go with you."

"No," I replied softly. "Stay with the rabble. I won't be far."

Frown lines appeared between her eyebrows for a fleeting moment, moonlight soft and blue across her cheeks, her lips. She squeezed my hand again. "Not far."

"Never." I leaned down and kissed her briefly, her mouth soft and yielding against mine. I knew if I lingered, I'd have to tell the moon rabbit and her shadow to scram so Lu and I could enjoy some privacy.

But the kiss was quick, and when I released her hand, her fingers trailed promises against my palm.

Lorde's ears twitched, and the dog opened her eyes, but didn't lift her head.

"Stay, girl. Guard Lu."

Lorde tapped her fuzzy tail against the pile of blankets she and Hado shared, but Lu huffed a soft laugh.

Lu had spent years keeping herself safe. Thanks to the attack, she was stronger than a human, and faster too. She was not a vampire, but had the same sharp hearing of one of those creatures, and had a slight aversion to long times in sunlight.

Didn't stop me from worrying about her.

I hauled my ass up onto the edge of the truck bed, then swung my legs over the other side, trying not to grunt and groan at the stiffness in every joint and bone.

My feet were bare, the left one asleep. There was no

chance I was going to stroll off into strange surroundings without my boots. I bent, fished my boots out from under the truck, leaving Lu's boots and Abbi's sneakers behind.

I shook out each boot—spiders and snakes were tricky jerks—then shoved my feet inside, not bothering to tie the laces.

I headed away from the truck toward the road instead of going deeper into the tree cover, the crunch of twigs and dry grasses crackling under my boots.

We'd fought monsters. Monster hunters too. I wasn't foolish enough to think we were safe. Not while we searched for the spell book of the gods Cupid had asked us to find.

And now we had Abbi and Hado to keep safe too.

I glanced back at the truck, a blur of silver in the darkness, and realized the moon rabbit and her shadow had done more than wriggle into the scant space of our truck. They'd also found a way into my heart.

I was fond of Abbi. Fond enough, I was beginning to think of her as family. But anyone close to Lula and me were targets for those people and creatures who wanted us dead.

The breeze lifted and fell, just enough to drag goosebumps down my neck.

Monster hunters, monsters like the Hush, and gods. There were too damn many of all of them meddling in the business of the human world.

Including Cupid, who had offered us a deal. I could be flesh and blood, Lu and I could both be alive, if we would help him bring a few people together, and help him find that stolen spell book of the gods.

We'd said yes, though we'd put in our exit strategy. At any time, we could call off the deal. He had our word, but not our loyalty. Never that.

l didn't trust gods. Didn't trust him.

I stopped at the edge of the rutted dirt road. We weren't too far off Route 66, but we'd pushed it a bit, wandering down a side road as far away from the old route as we dared.

Here under the open sky, it felt like I was an ocean away from any other living being.

I had lost sight of the truck, but I knew Lu was still awake, tracking the sound of my movements.

I inhaled, exhaled, and planted my hands on my hips, staring eastward, where the sky had begun to lighten.

What a life.

I didn't think it was one we were going to continue for long. No, the right thing, the best thing, would be to tell Abbi to hop on back up to the moon and tell Hado to look after her.

Tell Cupid we were done searching for the spell book.

Working for a god would only get people I cared about killed, and I didn't want any part of that. Our destiny, our future, only contained two things: finding the monsters who had attacked us near 100 years ago. And killing them.

The soft brush of wings above me drew my gaze, searching for the bird. It swooped down from the tree to my left, white, soft, feathers and a flash of gold eyes passing inches above my head, then off, out, down the road.

Owl, for certain. Screech owl? No, barn owl more likely.

I checked the trees for more, but when I glanced back down the road, a figure was walking my way.

She—I was almost sure it was a woman—had not been there a second ago. Yet she walked as if she had been hiking at this steady pace for hours.

I stepped back away from the road, into the darkness. There was no reason to draw attention to myself. No reason for her to know Lu and the others were just a little farther off in the field.

I could just keep backing away, let this midnight traveler travel along, but my conscience twigged. It wasn't even dawn. She was alone. Why would she be out here alone?

Car accident? Lost? Kidnapped? Injured?

I sighed and scratched at the welts on my neck and ear. I'd see if she needed help. That's all. Then I'd send her on her way.

Before I could move toward her, she called out.

"Hey there!" Her voice carried soft and low, like a mourning dove. She raised her hand and waved, bracelets rattling down from wrist to elbow. "I need to talk to you. You there. I see you!"

"'Course," I muttered more to myself, and maybe to Lu, if she was listening with those sharp ears of hers. I strolled out of the brush onto the road, stuck my hands on my hips. "How can I help you?"

She was older than I'd thought. Her white hair drawn away from her round face like carded wool that bunched and puffed. Wrinkles fanned the corners of her button eyes, folding down her knobby cheeks to bracket her mouth. Her nose and chin stuck out in a way that said she'd spent a lifetime standing her ground and speaking her mind.

"Do you need help?" I repeated.

"Me?" she asked, a little out of breath. "Oh, no, dear, not me. Not me at all." She stopped and twisted at the waist, looking at the fields on both sides of the road like she wasn't sure where we were.

She wore practical clothes: trousers under a skirt that draped to mid-calf, and sensible hiking boots. Her coat was too large, full of bulging pockets, and she had several shirts layered beneath it.

But it was her jewelry that caught my eye. Beads, mostly, strings of them, around her neck, her arms, her ankles. Some round and soft, but other rougher shapes of wire wrapped stone, wood, shell.

All of it together gave her a sound, a song. Beads clacked like spring rain on a hollow log, wood and shell hushed like dry leaves shifting in an autumn wind. She was rivers and birdsong, the soft poetry of the world.

"Are you all right?" I asked, falling into the sound she carried around her, wanting more of it, sure there were voices, pipes and drums just on the edge of my hearing.

"I am now." She planted her hands on her hips and nodded. "I've been looking for you, Brogan Gauge. You and Lula. And now I don't have much time. I blame you for that. You couldn't have stayed on the Route to make it easy for me?"

Chills ran down my arms and tightened the skin between my shoulder blades. She appeared human. But I was pretty sure she was not.

If not human, what kind of monster, creature, or god was she?

"I don't know what you're talking about." I stepped backward, wanting space, wanting room between her and me. Wanting space between her and my people in the truck.

She didn't move, didn't lift a damn foot. She sure as hell didn't take a step. Yet she was still right there in front of me—drawn forward as I moved backward—just as close as if I'd never moved.

"Of course you don't know what I'm talking about. You haven't met me yet. But when you do, you'll understand. There are things I need, and things you need even though you won't like it when you find out. But then, you might. You might like this, Brogan Gauge." She sucked a tooth and tipped her head to one side, considering me.

"What are you?" I knew ghosts. I didn't like them, but I could recognize one from half a state away. This woman, or whatever she was, was not a ghost.

Didn't look like a god either. I had a knack for knowing when a god was around. Both Lula and I had always been good at spotting god power.

But that didn't mean it was impossible for a god to fool us, to find a way to hide their power from our sight. There were a lot of trickster gods roaming the world.

"What am I?" She chuckled. "I forgot we do this. It's been, well, time doesn't matter, does it? Until it does, and then. Of course. Of course. Then it will matter. But until then…"

She leaned forward and peered up at me. Like a bird staring up a tree.

No, like an owl sighting prey.

"I am your future." She grinned and there was a jack-o'-lantern gap in her front teeth. "Well, I'm your now, too, now. Currently, is what I'm saying. We'll meet. You'll understand. Just don't skip the pop, all right? Stop at the pop and it's all going to make sense."

I ignored all that, since none of it made any sense. "Are you a god?"

Her eyes went wide, setting off an accordion of lines up her face from chin to forehead.

"Oh." She choked back a laugh. "No. No, not at all. Do I *look* like a god to you? I thought you could tell what a god looks like in any form. Aren't you *that* Brogan Gauge?"

"Ma'am," I said. "I don't know you, and you sure as damn don't know me. Just because you used my name doesn't mean I believe you are some kind of mind reader."

"That is true. Also, I am not."

"Not?"

"A mind reader," she said. "Or a god. Or…" she held both palms up and wiggled them, as if she had eggs between her fingers, "…whatever you might think I am. Do we really have to do this?"

Before I could answer, she said, "Yes, I know we do,

it's just. Well, let's get this rolling. Pop. Don't be late for your cue." She pointed one crooked finger at me and closed one eye, as if she was looking down a scope.

"I am not going to go anywhere—" The rest of what I was going to say—I won't be late because I plan to never see you again. I think you better back the hell off and leave me and mine alone—was cut short.

She was gone.

There was no woman. There was no rattle of beads. There was no song of woods and winds. Just a lonely dirt road jagging out into the dark of the night.

I scanned the fields, the trees, kneeled and inspected the dirt. No footprints except my own.

The cry of a barn owl, eerie and hawk-like, echoed against the stars. I tipped my eyes skyward, and caught the watercolor smudge of feathers, white, soft, and a flash of gold heading west, away from dawn's horizon.

CHAPTER TWO

"She's a shapeshifter?" Lu asked.

"I didn't say that." My head was pounding, the vision—or whatever that meeting had been with the woman—leaving behind a headache I couldn't shake.

"She turned into an owl," Lula said.

"Owls eat rabbits," Abbi noted.

"I didn't say she turned into an owl."

"But they do." Abbi looked up at me, dark eyes wide and sincere. "I like them anyway. They have moon faces."

Abbi sat on a bench inside the little gazebo they'd set up in what was now a park, right in the middle of a bunch of old buildings in Galena, Kansas. It used to be a garage and gas station, but once Howard "Pappy" Litch had passed on, they'd knocked the garage down and turned it into a park to honor the avid local historian.

It was a good choice, and a good place. I think Pappy would be pleased to see it.

He'd also be pleased the Streetcar Station Coffee shop was right across the street, and that they made the best damn homemade cinnamon rolls too.

Abbi's mouth and cheeks were still sticky with cinnamon and frosting. She'd followed the pastry with a fussy bite of scrambled egg, then quickly passed those to Hado and Lorde, who were lounging on the gazebo's wooden floor.

Lu tore off a bit of pastry, popped it in her mouth, then leaned back against the bench, licking the sugar off the tips of her fingers, one by one. The early morning shadows couldn't extinguish her copper hair, pale smooth skin, or tiger eyes. I could spend a lifetime looking at her.

Had already done so.

Her lips ticked up at the corner, a secret smile just for me.

"Come sit down." She patted the bench seat next to her. "Go through the important parts again. Explain how she wasn't a shapeshifter."

I was leaning against the gazebo railing, looking out at the empty road. Route 66 elbows into Kansas for a very short thirteen miles before shaking out across Oklahoma. Along those thirteen miles are three small towns: Galena, Riverton, and Baxter Springs.

Galena was a small town, only about three thousand residents. It had staked its claim on the Route by restoring a Kan-O-Tex service station, putting vintage cars on display—including the kind used in that Disney movie—commissioning a mural, and adding historic markers at interesting points along the way, like the park we were currently enjoying.

"Brogan," she said, gently, coaxing. "Sit. We're fine."

I gave in and pushed off of the post, then dropped down next to her.

"It wasn't a dream," I said.

"I know. You would have had to have gotten some sleep for it to be a dream."

I frowned. "It wasn't a hallucination, if that's what you're saying."

"Loud voice," Abbi mumbled around a mouth full of food.

"I'm not loud—"

Lu's hand dropped on my shoulder, and she squeezed the tight muscles there. The sound I made, something along the lines of a rubber tire being punctured, made her smile.

"Maybe a little loud," she said. "Just…rest a minute. I'll keep watch."

"I don't need to rest."

She hummed, and her hand moved to the back of my neck. She kneaded tight muscles and I closed my eyes and hung my head. I didn't care what sounds I was making.

"The thing about being alive?" Her voice was barely louder than the breeze through the trees, the snore of traffic somewhere at the edge of the world. "Is you have to caretake your body. Food. Water. Sleep." She leaned in, lips so close her breath stirred my hair when she whispered: "Desire."

I full-body shuddered in pure pleasure.

"Rest," she breathed.

I mumbled something that might have been a protest, but I didn't wait to see if it landed.

Sitting there, my arms crossed over my chest, head leaned forward, and Lu's hand on my back, I drifted.

Lorde growled and snarled a warning *woof*.

Lu's fingers gripped my shoulder a little tighter. A warning.

I heard Lorde's claws as she stood.

"Gauge?" the man said, his voice thin from surprise. "Lula? Are you Lula Gauge?"

Lorde growled again, deep in her chest. She wasn't attacking. Not yet.

I lifted my head and got a look at the speaker.

White man. Suit jacket and slacks, sunglasses. He was average height, plain unremarkable features, his sandy hair parted on the side and combed back with something that made it stiff.

He held a takeout coffee cup with a brown sleeve in one hand, and a trombone in the other. The trombone was dull, plain, but the mouthpiece was a beautiful scrollworked brass that shone.

"And you are?" I asked.

That was when he seemed to notice me. His eyes went wide. "Brogan?" The word pulled out of him like he'd lost all his breath.

"Do I know you?" I stood. Lu had her hand on Lorde's head, keeping our very faithful dog from launching at the—whatever or whoever he was.

I'd been a spirit, invisible to this world for almost a hundred years. Anyone who could recognize me on sight had to be supernatural in some way. It wasn't like any of our friends or contemporaries were still alive.

"We were…" He swallowed, and lifted his hand to remove his sunglasses, but forgot he held a brass instrument and clonked himself on the cheek. "Shit. Brogan." He tried the other hand and managed to get the glasses off without spilling his drink.

His eyes were the color of cardboard and set just a little too close together, which gave him a pinched, mean look.

"Matthew," he said. "Matthew Davis. How are you… How are you alive? Look at you." He had to swallow again and tears glittered at the bottom of his eyes.

"Matthew Davis." Lu stood but didn't offer him her hand. "I don't recall that name."

"You do," he insisted, "you do. We were young together. Back before…" He clamped his mouth shut and took a step back. "No. You shouldn't be here."

"In Kansas?" I asked.

"In now. In the here. You should be old. You should be dead. What are you?" He took another step back and missed the doorway he'd walked through when he'd entered the gazebo. He bumped into the gazebo railing behind him.

The street was empty, the shops quiet, the air growing heavy with the rising heat of the day.

It seemed normal. It all seemed right. But there was something off about this, and something very off about him.

"We're just going about our business. You should

too," I said. "Move along, stranger." I took a step, and he knocked his heel into the half wall, having somehow forgotten the railing behind him.

"She ran a bakery," he blurted, pointing his cup at Lula. "You worked odd jobs until she hired you. You were going to get married. Did that ever happen? Did you actually marry or did something happen that day? I seem to remember something happened."

Lu and I both went still. He was talking about our past, about our lives, like he'd been there.

"I asked nice," I said. "Now I'm not going to ask nice." I made a fist, and the satisfying sound of my knuckles cracking sent a sheet of sweat across the man's pasty face.

"Who are you?" Lu asked, before I could get to swinging.

"I told you. Matthew Davis. Years ago, I was a banker. I worked for the bank. Worked my way up. Your father took out his first business loan with our establishment. You came by and asked for a loan once—"

"And you said no," she replied.

I wouldn't say she relaxed. There was a wariness Lu carried with her now, refreshed with every breath she took. The world was a dangerous place for monsters like her. For monsters like me.

For monsters like him. Because this guy was too old in years and too young in face to be human.

Pasty and panicked in his nice suit, carrying a trombone of all things, he could be a monster hunter.

"Still don't recall your name," I said.

"Mad Mat," Lu said.

That name, I remembered.

He gave a sharp, startled smile. "I haven't heard that name in…well, in a lifetime."

"Or two," I said. I didn't want to believe her, didn't want to believe him. But if Lu was right, and this chump wasn't trying to play us as rubes, then we had another problem on our hands.

Mad Mat Davis, back when he had been human, had also been a snake in the grass, a real nasty piece of work.

"You remember, though. You remember me?" he asked.

"Sure, pal," I said. "Whatever you say."

His smile cracked, and through it bled a burning darkness that was felt, not seen. God power. Some time in his long life, he'd been touched by a god, marked. He may not even know it had happened. Many mortals were blessed, or cursed.

But just as quickly as I saw, or rather, felt the shock of what lingered behind his façade, it was gone.

He once again looked like a bookish, or maybe a banker-ish man, who was just as surprised as we were to stumble head-first into his impossible past.

"I, well, I remember both of you. And here you are. Alive. After all these years. May I…can I sit with you? Even if it's just for a short time?"

There was a bench next to him, which would put him across the gazebo from us. Lula nodded toward it, and he lowered down. She settled back onto our bench while I remained on my feet.

Abbi, who had been quiet all this time, clambered up to stand on the bench next to Lula.

"Oh," Mad Mat said. "Hello, little girl. You shouldn't stand on that. You might fall and damage yourself."

Abbi pursed her lips and squinted. "I see better from up high."

Of course she did. She was used to looking down at people from the moon.

Hado, who still looked like a little black cat, picked his way across the wooden floor to sit in the very center of the gazebo and stare unblinkingly at Mat.

"Explain yourself," I said. "We're listening."

He tipped his head, and it wasn't like a bird searching the sky. It was like a marksman sighting the bullseye.

"I don't remember you having such shabby manners," he sniffed.

And there it was. The condescending tone the years had all but scrubbed from my memory. The full memory of him flooded my mind. Him in his fine suits of the day, behind the expensive oak desk, his sneer as he decided who would get money to survive, and who would walk out of his office with no future ahead of them.

I remembered his strut, the pleasure that oozed out of him as he lorded over life after life. As if killing, even if it was once removed, twice removed, was what fed him. He just obscured his weapons of choice with terms like "credit" and "equity" and "market value".

"Time changes a man," I said. "Some men."

"Yes." He frowned. "So it can. Tell me," here his gaze ticked back to Lu, "how are you still alive?"

"Are you a man?" Abbi asked. "A real man?"

Annoyance tightened his eyes. "Of course I'm a man. Just like you're a little girl. A real little girl, right?"

"O-ka-y," she said, drawing the word out into three syllables. "Old man *and* mean." She hopped down off of the bench. "Hado, let's go play."

"Stay close," I admonished, like I was her father and she was actually a little girl.

She made a face at me and zipped off through one of the gazebo openings. I needn't have worried about her.

For one thing, she was a moon deity. For another, Hado followed her. And for the last, she jogged only a short way out into the grass. Then she spun in lazy circles, her arms stuck out straight, fingers splayed to catch the breeze.

"Is she…" he asked, the question heavy with implication. I could interpret the question many ways: Is she ours? Is she mortal? Is she aware of what Lu and I really were?

"You start." Lu, cool and collected, rested one booted foot on her knee and draped her arm across the back of the bench, her pale, thin fingers on the smooth wood. Her other hand was low, touching top of Lorde's furry head.

Lorde stared at Mat, her ruff still bristled, but she was no longer growling.

"Start?" He frowned. "Oh, you mean why I…um… look this way?"

"Sure," she said.

"It's a long story, really, and I don't claim to have been in the right of…well, anything I did. Most people don't believe me. That I'm…" he gestured to his face and body, "…as old as I am. A hundred years." He lifted his cup toward thin lips and grimaced before setting it on the bench. "You believe me, though, right?"

"It doesn't matter if we believe or not," I said. "It's your story." I didn't want to accept he was who he said he was. Did he look like Mad Mat? Yes. Did he talk like him and act like him? Yes.

But there had been that moment, that split second, when I thought he had been changed by something more, something darker.

Something powerful.

It had been the briefest glimpse, and felt like god power. But he could be a wizard casting an illusion spell. Or a monster that mimicked, or hell, maybe he was Mad Mat's grandson.

Who he was mattered. Mattered a lot.

But why he had zeroed in on us, why he had *suddenly* crossed paths with us here in this little town, now, was the real mystery.

He considered me for a moment, then plucked at the coffee lid with his fingernail, making little plastic popping noises. "I suppose. It is my story. But I am… can't I just say I'm grateful to share it with someone who might understand?" Here he gave me a wry smile and shrugged one shoulder. "Because I am. Grateful."

My gut tightened. There was a calculation in his gaze, as if he were holding a match and measuring how long the flame could chew the wick before the bomb exploded.

"I was a vain man in my youth." His cardboard gaze flicked to Lu and stalled there. "You remember, don't you, Lula? My righteousness? How I held myself above others as if I were superior? As if I were a king?"

When she didn't respond, he continued. "I regret those days. Things could have been…very different. For me. For you. We would have made a wonderful team."

I snarled.

He hunched his shoulders as if trying to hide. "In business. We would have made a wonderful business team. Remember, Lula? We could have expanded your bakery and sandwich shop. New locations. Franchises. What a thing that would have been. What a very fine thing."

His voice was soft, melodious, as if he had pondered this very dream for many, many years.

"You refused my loan," Lu said flatly.

"Well, you refused me, didn't you?" he retorted.

That was news to me. Although not a surprise. Lu was beautiful, smart, and courageous. I hadn't known why every man wasn't fighting to get to her back then.

I didn't know why they weren't fighting for her attention now.

She held her silence and his gaze.

He shifted, warming to the challenge in her stare, all the lines of him unwinding. Seemed like he was made of spring and coil and tension rods, and someone had just applied oil.

"Well, that is water under a very old bridge," he said

with a smile I did not like. "I should have partnered with you and your business. I know that now. We would have taken the world by storm. We would have been so profitable. Can you imagine what we could have done if we had given in just a little? Negotiated toward our common good?"

Lu planted both boots wide and leaned forward. "I have places to be, Mr. Davis. Goodbye." She made to stand.

"I was hunted," he blurted, all the gears of him suddenly spinning, as if the movie had gone into fast-forward and he had to get through half a show before the tub of popcorn was down to salt and seeds. "I didn't know it then, but I'd caught the attention of someone. Someone very dangerous."

Lu eased back a fraction, waiting.

He wiped his hand over his mouth, again forgetting he had a damn trombone in it, and nearly clocked himself in the nose. He glared at the instrument, then set it down on the floor beside him.

"I had begun collecting antiquities," he said, a little calmer. "Some that were brought back from the wars, others I researched and, through extensive contacts, procured. My business moved from banking to banking and collection. I enjoyed the thrill of finding rare items, enjoyed holding them, or in the rare cases, selling them for large amounts. Astounding amounts.

"But it was never the money that drove me. It was the hunt. I attracted the attention of the wrong people. I became the hunted."

He lifted the cup and pulled a long swallow, then

wiped lips with the tips of his fingers, his gaze lost to the past. "I thought I had caught the attention of aggressive collectors, but it was more than that, worse than that."

"Mob?" I asked.

He licked his lips. "That's what I thought. Powerful men with a thirst to control the weak. To claim what wasn't theirs and kill anyone in their way. But there were darker forces." He leaned in, and I could see the sweat spilled across his face. It gave him a sickly sheen. "Supernatural forces."

"Like ghosts?" Lu's voice dripped with doubt. "Aliens?" And oh, the judgement she packed into that.

He sat back, his spine straight. "You don't believe me."

"I believe you are telling the story you want to tell."

"How else?" His voice rose. "How else, except through magic, could I still be alive? Still be this young?"

"About that," I said. "You've assumed we believe you are who you say you are."

"How else would I have recognized you? How else could I have told you those details—the loan, the bakery. Our past?"

"We never said we are who you assume we are," Lu said simply.

"Fine." He stuffed a hand into his jacket pocket and pulled out a palm-sized silver mirror, the back of which was worked into the shape of a woman's face. She had waves of hair bound in a manner that was in fashion back when tales of Zeus were being told by shepherds.

There was magic in the mirror. I could feel it from across the gazebo.

"This truth I will know, this truth I will give," he recited, holding the mirror up close enough his breath fogged it.

He turned it toward us, and light flashed, star-bright and blinding.

"Are you Lula and Brogan Gauge?"

I clamped my jaw and breathed hard against the compulsion to speak.

"Yes," Lu said. She did not sound happy about it.

He spun the mirror on himself. "Am I Mathew Davis, born nineteen-oh-eight?"

The same flash of light hit him. He winced, then answered: "Yes."

It shouldn't make a difference, him saying the same thing he'd been saying all along, but hearing him admit it under the mirror's magic made me realize it was true.

Well, shit.

"You can tell," he said, wearily. "You can tell I am not lying. Just as I know you are not lying. We," he pocketed the mirror, leaving the lemon tang of magic behind, "are of a kind, the three of us. Three of a kind." He slumped against the bench, as if he'd just run a long distance in a very short time.

He closed his eyes and rubbed at them.

I uncrossed my arms and hung my hand, tipping it slightly, knowing Lu would understand. *Time to go?*

I knew her answer, because she got to her feet. "We aren't anything of a kind," she said. "Goodbye, Mr. Davis."

He bolted up and took two steps our way. I put my big body in front of Lu, Lorde moving fast to stand by my side, growling.

"Back down and back off," I said. "This conversation is over."

He'd left the coffee and trombone on the bench, his hand clutching something in his pocket.

Did he have a weapon there? Something with more powerful magic than the mirror?

I reached for his arm, my big mitt closing around his wrist.

Lorde growled, ears flat, teeth bared.

Mad Mat took another step, that crack of a smile dripping darkness like this was some sort of game he was winning.

Then Abbi screamed.

CHAPTER THREE

Lu was gone, a liquid shadow, a blur, already out onto the grass where Abbi lay curled on her side, crying.

Mad Mat didn't look her way, but that strange smile went broken and wild.

Hungry. He was hungry for this. Wanted this fight. "Do you really think she's yours?" he rasped. "Do you really think you can keep her from me?"

I didn't know if he was asking about Abbi or Lu, but my answer was the same. "Yes."

I increased the pressure on his wrist until I felt his bones bend.

He only smiled wider.

A truck took the corner, the big engine chugging as it rumbled by, and that noise seemed to shake something in his gaze back into place.

Sanity, I thought.

Mat dropped the smile and stepped back.

"That was…unfortunate." He stared at his feet, red

slapped across his pale cheeks. "I had wanted… But no, that was inappropriate of me. All these years, I have a bit of a hair trigger. My apologies. This will take time. I know this will take time.

"We could meet somewhere. We could talk again. I promise not to…" He shrugged, but didn't try to pull his hand away. He just stood there, passive.

I fought the urge to punch him until that strange smile of his turned to dust. I fought the urge to turn him around and give him the bum's rush.

But Abbi was still crying, and I'd already wasted enough time on this joker.

"Leave me and mine alone," I said. "That is your only warning. I see you again, and I will reduce you to hash. Understand?"

His eyes flicked up. There was anger there, but he quickly dropped his gaze again. "Yes."

I squeezed his wrist just that much harder, felt bones shift. He hissed, but made no move to pull away.

I released his arm and strode past him out to the grass. Lorde wasn't done snarling and threatening, but I snapped my fingers and she left him to come to my side.

"She hurt her ankle." Lu's hand wrapped gently around Abbi's bare foot, the other hand supporting the weight of her leg.

Abbi was curled like a leaf, hugging Hado and making small, pitiful sounds.

"Does she need a doctor?" I asked.

It wasn't panic that made my words a little too high. Couldn't be panic that crumpled my lungs and soured my stomach. There wasn't any need to panic.

Abbi wasn't actually a child. Wasn't nearly as fragile as she looked. And yet, I found it hard to breathe through the tightness in my chest.

"Should I go for a doctor?" I asked again. "I can find one. Someone in the coffee shop should know. I'll be quick." I got half a step away when Abbi stuttered out one last sob.

"Is he gone?" she asked.

Lu raised an eyebrow and glanced up at me.

I gave her a blank look.

"Mad Mat," she said.

Why was Lu smiling now? Why was she looking at me like I was the most interesting thing she'd ever seen?

"Brogan?" she prompted.

"Right." I scanned the park, the gazebo, the empty street, and shop windows. "There's no one. No Mat."

Abbi snuffled. "He's g-gone?"

"He's gone."

Abbi rolled onto her back, her arms out at her side, gaze on the sky. Hado, still snuggled on her chest, head-butted her chin. "Good," she said. "He was awful. Can we have more cinnamon rolls?"

Lu rocked back on her heels, her eyebrows raised. "I take it you're not really hurt?" She stood up out of her crouch and planted hands on her hips. "Abbi, are you hurt?"

"No." She blinked up at both of us and her dark, wide eyes and chubby face were utterly tear-free. "I just wanted him to leave."

"Abbi," Lu admonished.

"You wanted him to leave too, didn't you?"

"That's not…" Lu tucked a strand of red hair behind her ear. "Yes, I wanted him to leave. But if you cry, I will believe you are injured. Brogan almost chased down a human doctor, and what do you think the doctor would have seen if he'd stuck you in an X-ray machine?"

"Rabbit bones?"

"Rabbit bones," Lula agreed. "And then we would have had to figure out how to fix that mess. We might have had to hurt people or destroyed machines."

Her mouth formed a perfect little "O." "I thought you could tell I was acting."

"We couldn't," Lu said.

Abbi grinned. "Because I'm such a good actor, right? That's why you believed me?"

"No more acting," I said on a held exhale. That had been a lot. The worry for Abbi had swamped me with adrenalin and it was going to take a while for it to bleed off.

"You believed me too," Abbi said to me. "I'm amazing!"

"You are not to do that again," Lu repeated.

"Lie or act?"

"Either," I said. "Just don't do either. Don't lie about being hurt," I added.

"Except when I really need to. Like when that old weird guy is trying to make you lose your temper and punch him, right?"

"I never lose my temper."

Lu gave me a wide-eyed look.

I felt the blush heat my face and neck. "Often," I

amended. "I don't lose my temper very often. And sometimes punching people is the way to fix things."

Lu pointed at Abbi. "No lying. No acting."

"All right," Abbi said. "But I'm sort of acting all the time." She grinned, and her nose twitched. The happy twinkle in her eyes was moon bright.

"Hello there!" a male voice called out. "You folks need any help?"

Bill, the owner of the coffee shop, stood on the sidewalk across the street. He was an older man who could tell a cracking good story and pour a cup of coffee that was so rich, I'd asked for a second before the first was done.

"We're good," I said, turning toward him.

He'd rolled up the sleeves of his green button down, and his balding head was bare to the sun. "Is your daughter all right, then?"

"She is, she is." I started his way, for no other reason than to work off some of the tension bottled up in me. "Just bumped her knees playing. You know how kids are."

"Sure," he said. "Little firecrackers full of energy."

"That's right," I said. "Thanks for asking, though. I appreciate it."

"Pleasure, pleasure. You folks planning to be around for lunch? We're making a goulash that will knock your hat off."

My stomach rumbled, but I gave another wave. "We have an appointment to keep out in Oklahoma," I lied, "and need to get going."

"We could order you up some to go."

I opened my mouth to say no again, but my stomach growled louder.

Lu was watching. I could feel her attention just like I had when I'd been a spirit. I'd know where she was, just as she'd know where I was, from half a state away.

We each carried a part of each other's soul.

Lula, my wife, my soul, was amused.

"How long would it take to box some to go?" I hedged, just to be polite. Just to be friendly.

The man's smile shone like a silver dime. "No time at all. Why don't you folks come back inside? It's nice and cool. We'll see if there isn't a little sweet for your girl there."

I flailed for an excuse. "Our dog and cat," I said to ward off the hour's long conversation I could see looming in my future if we got corralled into his shop.

"Both welcome, if they're well behaved. That's a real pretty dog you got there. Part chow chow you said?"

I glanced back at Lorde, who sat next to Lu. Lu's smile softened. It was the kind of smile that let me know I was all hers, and she was happy about it.

Abbi was bouncing on the balls of her feet, eyes wide and hopeful. The little black cat, who was not a little black cat, draped over her shoulders, a darker shadow beneath her shaggy white hair.

I raised an eyebrow. Lu nodded.

"That's right," I said to Bill. "Part chow chow and shepherd." I snapped my fingers softly.

Lorde ran on over and leaned against my leg, pushing her big fuzzy head under my hand so I could give her a scrub. I dragged fingers behind her soft ears while she huffed and made happy little yawning noises. "She's a very good girl."

"Well, bring her on in," he said. "I have a bowl of water and a choice ham hock for her. You have a few minutes, right?"

Lu and Abbi made their way to us, and Lu dropped her hand next to mine. I took her hand as I always would, weaving my fingers between hers.

"We have a few minutes," I said. Lu squeezed my hand.

"We have *all* the minutes," Lu said.

"Mat Davis?" The coffee shop proprietor had his big hands curled around the takeout containers filled with goulash. We'd been ready to leave a half hour ago, but he was still holding our lunch as soft hostages, keeping us in the quiet shop to visit a while longer.

It was a technique well used by gossips, the curious, and the lonely. I was pretty sure Bill was a little bit of all three.

"Mr. Davis doesn't live here. Well, not now. His family had a house out somewhere in Topeka, I heard."

"But he does business here?" Lu asked.

"Oh, I suppose." Bill let go of one container to open the paper bag that had been lying on the counter undisturbed for some time now. "He's one of those antique collectors, you know. I think they called them pickers for a while, but really, he's just finding old junk, shining it up, and selling it online."

That explained the trombone. It probably also

explained the magic mirror in his pocket, though it didn't explain how he knew how to use the mirror.

"Isn't that something," Lu said. "I've done a bit of that over the years."

"Have you?" His hands stilled, the paper bag yawning and empty.

Abbi sat on a wooden stool, swinging her feet. She got up and hummed her way toward the big front window like no one could see what she was doing.

She was up to something. I knew she was.

"I have a few old things in storage," Bill said. "If you have the eye for this sort of thing, maybe you'd want to take a look?"

Lu tipped her head. "If Mr. Davis has been through it, I'm sure he's taken the most valuable items."

"Who said I let him look through my storage? I'd rather save my valuables for someone with a good head on her shoulders." Bill gave her a wink, and my Lu, who could stare down the gods themselves, went pink beneath her freckles.

I camped back on one foot and grinned, enjoying her discomfort, so rarely shown to others.

"Now," he went on. "I understand you have places to be. Oklahoma, I think you said." He gave the bag a shake, like that would make any difference for the insertion of our rapidly cooling lunch.

"We do," Lu said with a slight hesitation. She might not have started life as a picker looking for lost treasures and hidden magics, but she'd been hooked on it for decades now. It'd been the primary way she'd funded her life on the road.

"Far be it from me to keep you away from your business," Bill said, fingers pinching the edge of the brown bag, the other hand still curled defensively around the food. "But if you wander back this way, I think you might find some very lucky things I'd be willing to part with. For the right price."

The door opened and a woman with the curliest hair I'd ever seen piled up on her head sauntered in. She wore blue shorts, a tan shirt, and a pair of very practical shoes. A mail bag slung across her chest.

"Morning, Bill." She gave Lu and I a nod. "Got your mail." She placed a handful of envelopes, including one that was roughly book shaped on the counter. "Buns still fresh?"

"Freshest buns in town!" He did a little hip bump to both sides, and the two of them grinned like this was a joke they were never gonna wear out.

"One and a fresh cup of coffee, cream?" he asked, already turning toward the case of fresh cinnamon buns behind him.

"Wouldn't hurt to get off my feet for a bit." She hoisted the bag and dropped it onto a chair, then sighed down into the other chair at the small table close to the counter. "You folks driving the Route?"

I raised my eyebrows. "That obvious?"

She shrugged. "It's the right time of year. You're not from around here, I'd guess, and Bill is giving you extra helpings of the goulash everyone in town fights over."

"Repeat business and good reviews are worth a little extra goulash. Plus, it can't be easy keeping that man of yours fed." He gave Lu another wink.

"I'm not that big of an eater," I argued. But my stomach growled and I slapped my hand over it.

Lu fought back a smile. "We manage. He's an easy keeper."

That drew a chuckle out of the old guy. Lu gave me a sly side-eye, and I scowled at her. She pressed fingers over her mouth to cover a cough that sounded suspiciously like a laugh.

"Owls," Abbi said, the glass making little pinging sounds as she poked the window with her finger. "A bunch of them."

"It's probably just a hawk, cutie," Bill said. "Owls are nocturnal. They're sleeping in the trees right now."

"It's not a hawk," Abbi said. "It's an owl...oh, it's two owls." She backed away from the window, fear all over her, her arms stiff and hands splayed at her side. She looked like she was trying to fade back into the protective shadows, inch by inch.

The mail carrier wasn't paying any attention. She'd pulled out her phone and was tapping at it with her thumbs.

"Three," Abbi breathed.

I crossed to her, and as soon as I stopped, she took my hand and held tight.

Hado was still on her shoulders. He growled softly, gray eyes glowing with a little too much light.

"Where?" I asked.

Abbi pointed.

I had to duck to see the sky from her line of sight. There, on the top of the gazebo across the street, was a barn owl. Another landed beside it.

Abbi's breathing grew quick, and she squeezed my fingers hard enough it hurt. "More," she whispered.

Another and another landed on the gazebo. Until there were five, six, eight, twelve.

"Lu," I said, keeping my tone easy. "I think it's time we be going."

She had miraculously wrested the bagged lunch away from Bill and was headed to the door.

Bill came out from behind the counter and put the plated cinnamon roll in front of the mail carrier. He ducked his head to get a view out the window.

"Will you look at that? You'd think it was some kind of omen or something. Wonder if a fire pushed them out of their roosts…"

I supposed that was as good an explanation as any, though it was not a fire that had sent those owls.

As soon as we stepped out of the shop, every owl turned its head to stare at us.

Yellow, gold, amber, ale, those eyes burned like a hundred eclipsed suns.

There was magic in those owls. There was power.

"Get to the truck," I said, turning our fast walk into a slow jog. "Just keep moving."

I patted my pocket for the keys, but Lu tapped my arm and sprinted ahead, the keys in her hand.

"They're coming," Abbi said. "Brogan, they're coming. They're coming for us!" Her voice rose and rose. I glanced behind my shoulder and saw why.

Every one of the owls was in flight, dream-silent and fast—nightmare-fast—swooping our way as if they were one wing, one creature, with a hundred claws extended.

I bent, scooped Abbi into my arms, and then put some pepper into my stride.

Lu made it to the truck before me, the door open, then in the driver's seat, the engine growling to life. I was only a step behind her, maybe three, but the ground under my feet had gone to sand, the air in my lungs cut like shards of glass.

I couldn't feel Abbi in my arms.

Something was wrong.

The truck, which had been so close, was somewhere out there at the end of a dark tunnel that stretched and stretched ahead of me.

Abbi said my name, but it was marshmallow soft, bouncing off my ears the minute she said it. I threw her toward the truck, hoping she would land on her feet, hoping she would make it to Lu.

Then the world dissolved into owl feathers and golden light.

"You usually give me three guesses," the woman said, "but this time, I'm only going to need one. Was it owls? I really hope it was owls."

I stood next to a gas pump, the parking area around me abandoned.

The woman on the other side of the gas pumps leaned her head between them and grinned at me, her wrinkles carving deeper and arrowing upward.

"I was going to say crows," she said, "because it was crows once, or maybe pigeons—which: messy. But I'm hoping we're on owl time, mostly because it's my favorite."

"Owls?" I asked. I hadn't been here a moment ago at this gas station, at any gas station. Where was Lu?

"She's fine. They're fine. All of them are fine." She waved her hand to one side, but the pumps hid her from my view. "Lula and the bunny. It's you and me here because you're the easiest for me to see in owl time."

She tottered out from behind the pump. She wore trousers beneath a skirt, and layers of shirts. Strings of beads wrapped her wrists, ankles. Around her neck hung bits of wood and wire. Metal, clay, and glass mumbled and clicked as she moved.

"You were in my dream," I said.

"That wasn't a dream, Brogan. You were wide awake and experiencing a vision. Just like now."

"Why? What do you want?"

She stopped about six feet from me and waved her hand over her shoulder at the building behind her. "Why? You are having a vision so you and I can talk. So I can guide you, inspire you. I didn't think I'd have to print out a program for you to follow along."

"Then get to it," I said. Time was never on my side when these things happened. For all I knew, I could have fallen into a coma and been sleeping for a decade. "What do you want?"

"I want you to find me. Same as I said before. Find me, Brogan."

"You've found me twice. Just say what you need to say."

"You think you know everything?"

I crossed my arms over my chest. "I know some things, yes."

"Do you know why the gods are watching you? Do you know why the moon fell to find you? Would you know a real monster if it spit in your eye? No. Because it already has and here you are, telling me you're dreaming."

"I know a trickster when I see one."

Her head jerked back, the poof of white curls bouncing. "Trickster?"

"Visions, promises, veiled threats. Posing as an old woman. You tick all the trickster boxes, so say your piece. Or I will break through this vision like a hammer on a fun-house mirror."

"If I could say my piece, do you think I would have sent owls after you? It was owls, wasn't it? That past is my favorite. You didn't even notice the pigeons. An entire flock coming at your head. How do you ignore an entire flock of pigeons?"

"I'm done." I walked straight at her. I'd been a spirit for most my years. I figured she was a spirit too. And one thing about spirits is they are not solid.

"Wait," she said, holding up both hands, like that could stop me. "I'm not—" She scuttled to one side, and I checked her shoulder as I kept going.

She "*oofed*".

She felt real; she felt solid. I hadn't expected that.

"You won't believe me here. No matter how many ways I try to say it." She chuckled and there was music in that laughter, pure delight that stilled my anger.

"I know you have muscles and a lot of stubbornness.

At least this isn't the time where you try to pick me up and toss me over the horizon. See where you are, where we are, Brogan Gauge."

The gas pumps were slightly behind me and to my left. In front of me was a building, white with floor-to-ceiling windows in front and a roofline that angled up, like a jet plane wing. It was a store, maybe a restaurant.

"Go ahead," the owl woman said. "Get a good look."

I turned a slow circle and spotted the sixty-six feet tall neon soda bottle attached to the building.

We were at Pops 66 Soda Ranch in Arcadia, Oklahoma, which is where she'd told me to meet her in the first vision.

I finished my turn, facing her. "Try," I said. "Tell me what I'll never believe."

She pulled her lips over her teeth and squinted at me. "All right. All right. I'll tell you. That god who found you isn't what he seems. He's not on your side. He's not helping you. And if you continue down this path, you will regret having anything to do with him. There." She stabbed a finger in the air in front of her. "Now that I've so much as mentioned it, he's gonna tear this vision to shre—"

The gas station exploded.

A wall of heat steamrolled across the pavement, stealing all my air and burning my lungs. I yelled—

—and stumbled.

I was running, the air thick with the algae green of a river under the afternoon sun. There was no fire, there was no explosion. Bird shadows swooped above me.

The disorientation set off panic, fear, and then just plain anger.

Anger always set me right.

I almost landed on the concrete face first, but caught myself on one knee and hand, and pushed back up.

This was not the gas station—

—*blue sky above*—

—this was not Oklahoma—

—*silver truck just ahead*—

—this was not an explosion—

—*Lu, half out of the truck, turned as if to run to me, sunglasses casting rose shadows over her eyes, one hand on the pocket watch she wore around her neck*—

—this was not a dream. Or a vision. This was reality. Now.

I slapped my hand against the truck's tailgate, and the vehicle rocked from the impact.

"Brogan?" Lu asked.

I pivoted, scanning the street behind me—empty, quiet, Streetcar café, gazebo in park, and all the rest just as it was—then the sky.

Nothing but blue. Not a single owl or bird to be seen.

I wiped my hand over my face, wicking away the sweat.

"Brogan?" she said again, moving my way.

"I'm good." I searched the sky again. "I'm okay. You saw the owls?"

She nodded. "Abbi got in the truck and you weren't with her."

"I was here?" That sounded strange, but she took it in stride.

"I didn't have eyes on you the entire time, but I didn't feel you go anywhere." She moved closer, took my hand. "What happened?"

"A drea—a vision."

"That owl woman? From the road last night?"

"Yeah."

Lu studied my face. She knew I was telling the truth.

She also knew I hadn't slept much last night. She knew other things too—that I'd been having nightmares ever since I'd been targeted by the Hush. That I was still new to this being alive thing.

That I could still see the ghosts who lingered here on earth, and importantly, that my perception of what was real might not be as reliable as someone else's.

She pressed her palm against my cheek. "Are you okay?"

I closed my eyes, reveling in her touch. Even though it had been two months since the god, Cupid, had gifted me with a physical body again, I still shivered under the overwhelming sensations of her, the richness of her touch.

"I am," I said, pressing my hand over hers. "Let's drive before we catch Bill's attention. I'll fill you in on what happened. We have a god problem."

CHAPTER FOUR

"Cupid doesn't like you?" Abbi asked again, for the fourth time, the sixth time, maybe the hundredth time.

"That's what the seer said," I repeated.

My headache from the vision was worse this time, cranking up to be a full-on migraine. The rumble from the truck's engine and jolting of the tires through pot holes weren't helping much.

Lu was trying not to appear worried about me, but she kept throwing quick glances my way, her fingers restless on the wheel, tapping, tapping.

"I'm fine," I assured her again. I propped one elbow on the frame of the door, and rested my head in my hand, eyes closed.

Lorde, who had scrunched up between Abbi and me, whined softly and draped more of her furry torso over my body.

Chevrolet hadn't had luxury in mind when they'd made this F-10 back in the 1960s. It was meant to be a working truck, strong and steady, and it did that well. But just at the moment, I was wishing for a headrest and a little more leg room.

"I'll find us a place and pull over," Lu said.

"But, Cupid?" Abbi piped.

"I'm fine," I said, though it came out a little raspy. "Just. Headache."

"I'll find us a place," Lu said.

"I liked Cupid," Abbi grumbled.

Abbi's voice was hard to hear over the stabbing pain in my brain. If the world would stop shaking, it would be okay. I would be okay. I had to be okay. I couldn't leave Lula after we'd just started our life together again.

"Brogan?" Lu sounded like she'd picked up a tin can and was using it as a telephone. "Bro—oh, shit. Hold on, love…"

The line went dead and blessed darkness smothered the pain in my head and dragged me down.

I WAS ON A BOAT. The sway and rock of waves was the first thing I noticed. I should smell the salt of water, or hear the creak of wood, but instead, I heard Lula.

"Set him here. Thank you. Yes. Careful."

A great wave rolled the ship, and cool sheets pressed against my skin.

"You need to swallow this," Lu said. "Brogan, open your eyes."

If there was a breath of will left in me, I would try to do what that woman asked of me. So I opened my eyes.

Not a ship, a room. Unfamiliar and mostly beige,

low light bleeding through closed blinds. The smell of dust and mustiness, with the slight tang of pine cleaner.

A motel.

"There you are." Her face came into view. She loomed above me, my love, my life, and her smile was soft, even though the lines between her brows sketched worry.

"Pain killers, good ones. Open your mouth, and swallow these with water, then you can go back to sleep."

Behind her stood Hado. He was no longer a little black cat. He was a large, stern looking dark-skinned man. He must have been the one who carried me out of the truck and dropped me onto the bed.

"I'm fi—" I started, but as soon as my mouth was open, she dropped a pill onto my tongue and held a plastic cup to my lips.

"Swallow," she said. "Pain killers."

The water was cool and refreshing and I drank it all down.

"It's just a headache," I whispered. "I'm fine, Lu."

"I know," she said, though the lines of worry were still there. "Sleep. You haven't been getting enough of that. I'll be here when you wake."

SOME CARTOON KID with a squeaky voice was having a heck of a time figuring out how to open a door, or maybe it was how to close a door. They had one goofy-voiced friend giving them advice that I could tell—even groggy and coming up out from under a flock of sheep —wasn't gonna do them any good.

"Righty tighty?" Abbi giggled. "What even is that?"

"Instructions," I tried to say, but it came out scratchy, so I cleared my throat and tried again. "How to open and close something."

I opened my eyes. The room hadn't gotten any less beige, but the light through the blinds had changed.

It was night again. I'd slept the day away.

"Hi." Abbi hopped off the other bed in the room and stood next to mine. "Lula told me to feed you more pain pills if you wanted them."

"I don't want them."

Abbi frowned, her bottom lip sticking out. "But she told me I was in charge of the pills."

I rubbed my hand over my face then grunted and groaned until I was sitting with my back to the headboard. The room swayed once, but I blinked until it steadied.

"My headache's better," I said.

Hado, standing by the closed door with his arms crossed over his chest, snorted.

"Maybe just one pill?" she begged. "It's small."

"No pills. Not even small ones."

She sighed dramatically. "Now I don't have a job. Can I sit next to you?"

I patted the thin comforter, and she jumped up onto the bed. "Lula is getting food. She left a few, yeah, a few minutes ago. She's not back yet. Did I wake you up with the TV?"

She wadded the blanket in her hands, getting it out of her way as she scooted closer.

"No. Not really."

She flashed me a smile and turned, putting her back to the headboard like me. Then she rested her head on my shoulder. She drew her knees up and stared at the TV bolted to the dresser on the other side of the room. "It's about keys," she said, "and doors."

"I see that."

We were both quiet for a bit while the cartoon friends figured out how to put a key in a lock and open the door, then made a big deal of walking back and forth across the threshold.

"I've been thinking about it," Abbi said. "About Cupid."

I did my best not to sigh. "I didn't say I believed the owl woman, Abbi," I said. "I was just repeating what she said."

"But she said god, right?"

"Yes."

"And that I fell to find you?"

"That too."

"But I don't think?" She twisted to look up at me. The show had gone to commercials and a woman in a crisply pressed shirt was sniffing some kind of deodorant like it was her wedding bouquet.

"I don't think I fell to find you. Please don't be mad." She bolted up, legs curled under her in a crouch, feet flat on the mattress. "I *might* have fallen to find you, but I don't remember. Maybe I just came down here to save Hado. And for the cookies."

There were times like this that Abbi seemed very much a child instead of the powerful being I knew she was. I glanced at Hado. His watery gaze was not at all human as he watched to see what I would do.

I straightened and scrubbed at my hair. It had been a day or two since I showered. I itched and probably stank.

"Are you angry I didn't fall for you?" she asked, sounding very young.

"No. Abbi, why would I be angry? I want you to listen to me, all right? Use those big ears of yours."

That made her smile, all teeth for a flash, before she went back to twisting the blanket between her fingers.

"I had a vision."

"Two."

"Yes. I had two visions. They were sent to me, or magicked on me by the owl woman, who I think is a seer or a trickster. Now, I might be wrong about both my guesses as to what she is.

"People are not always what they look like. Magical people are not always who they say they are. For instance, a ten-year-old girl with shaggy white hair and big eyes, who likes cookies…"

"…loves."

"…who loves cookies, might actually be a deity. The Moon Rabbit. And her fuzzy little kitten might actually be her shadow and protector, who is sometimes a big grumpy man."

That smile again, quick, but there were still clouds in her eyes. "But it *was* a vision," she said. "Visions are important. Like magic. Like dreams."

"Yes, all those things are important. But this vision was more of a place where one woman—if she was a woman—wanted to talk to me. She might be telling the truth, or she might be lying about everything."

Abbi nodded. "But if she's telling the truth, then I fell to find you, but I don't know why I would do that." She lifted her chin at an angle, and closed one eye, peering at me like an insect she'd never seen before. "What's so important about you?"

I yawned and scrubbed my head again. "I have no idea. Like I said, just because it was a vision, doesn't mean it's the truth."

The door handle clacked with a key being inserted into it—none of those fancy keyless entries at this place, apparently.

"Oh! The chain." Abbi sprang off the bed and pinched the chain between her fingers. "Is that you, Lula?"

"You can look through the peephole to make sure."

"I know your voice. I heard you coming. And I heard Lorde too."

"Still," Lu said, "it's always good to check."

Abbi did as Lu suggested and looked through the peephole. "It's you. And it's Lorde. And you have food." She unlatched the chain.

"He wouldn't take any of the pills but I did good watching him," she said as Lu walked in with several bags, one that might have groceries, but another that was definitely Chinese food.

"You did." Lu's attention was on me, gauging how I was feeling.

"Thanks a lot," I said, doing my best to look annoyed.

Lu blinked, and her eyebrows rose. "For?"

"Making me have to decide between a shower and whatever it is that smells like heaven in that bag."

"Orange chicken."

"Gods damn, woman."

That pulled a smirk out of her. "Shower, and I might save you some." She carried the bags over to the dresser and set them there.

Abbi was already digging through one before it was out of Lu's arms.

Lorde trotted over to the bed and stuck her big fuzzy head on the mattress, soft brown gaze on me, curled tail wagging. I stroked behind her silky ears.

"Good girl, looking after Lu for me."

Her tail wagged faster.

I stroked her head, then pushed the blankets away and gave my feet a try. Lorde stepped backward as I moved forward, as if she was making sure I wasn't going to fall.

"A taste?" I asked Lu, who handed Abbi one of the white cartons and paper-wrapped chopsticks.

Lu plucked up a new set of chopsticks, dug around in the carton, and offered a glossy orange chunk of chicken.

The room was small, most of it taken up with the beds. It took all of two steps to put me within her reach. I opened my mouth and bit the chicken off the chopsticks.

A burst of savory, sweet, salty, hit me like a meteor

strike. Eating, tasting food, was still a treat that could knock me off my feet.

"Shower can wait." I crowded up in her space and made a move on the carton of chicken.

She batted at my hands. "No. You stink."

"We all stink." I feinted toward the rice, but she turned her shoulder and back on me, not falling for my ruse.

"Abbi showered while you were sleeping. Step it up, Brogan. Faster you bathe, faster you get food."

"You aren't in charge of the rules," I said.

"I am in charge of this food." She shifted her grip on the chopsticks, holding them like a weapon. "Soap. Water. We'll all be the better for it."

I changed my plan of attack and reached out, my hand on her hip. "Hey, baby. That's some good-looking chicken you got there. How about we curl up in bed, put on a movie, and you let me put my chopsticks to some good use?"

She laughed and pushed me away. "Terrible. Go."

I'd seen the little blush under her freckles, and that made me feel pretty good about myself.

I thought I'd be quick in the shower, but once I got the water to the right temperature, I lingered, the spray working out knots in my neck and shoulders.

The bathroom was steamed up by the time I stepped out and dried. I wiped off the mirror, thought about a shave, and decided the scruff could wait until morning. Or maybe I just wouldn't shave for a while.

I wrapped the towel around my waist and strolled out of the bathroom.

Hado was back in kitten form, curled up on the other bed with Abbi, who drank water from a clear plastic cup.

Lu had kicked off her boots and sat on the bed where I'd been sleeping, one foot on the floor, one bent beneath her. Lorde snoozed at the bottom of the bed. Her food bowl was empty and her water bowl was lower than it had been.

Lu's gaze did a slow pan up my body. From the heat in her gaze, I knew she wasn't searching me for signs of injury.

I had to do some backwards counting to keep my reaction under control.

Mercy, what that woman could do to me.

"Ready to eat?" she asked.

I might have followed that up with flirting, but my stomach rumbled. "I could eat. Let me pull on some pants."

Lu had stopped unpacking in motel rooms years ago. Mostly because when I was in spirit form, she rarely stayed in motels.

She'd been living out of a duffle bag for so long, it was more than a habit to keep it packed and ready. It was a way of life. It was the way of the road.

We'd bought an extra duffle for me, and it gave me a little ping of happiness to see my duffle resting next to hers.

Tossed on top of both of ours was Abbi's bright blue backpack. It was unzipped and had obviously been rummaged through, leaving striped shirts and polka dot tights spilling out like colorful flowers.

Seeing all our bags there in a tumble together was almost, I thought with a strange sense of satisfaction, what a family looked like.

It made something settle in me. Something I'd given up on decades ago.

I cleared my throat against the emotions I wasn't ready to name and grabbed my bag. I took it with me to the bathroom, since I had no desire to flash my moon to the lunar bunny.

Dressed, I stepped back into the main room. Lu frowned at her phone.

"Trouble?" I dropped my duffel and eased onto the bed next to her, snagging up the carton she'd set on the side table.

The orange chicken glistened, a sweet, salty mess. I settled the chopsticks between my fingers and dug in.

"Headwaters." She tipped the phone so I could read the text.

I chewed and swallowed. "He wants you to call. Why are you worried?"

She shrugged and set the phone on the table between the beds. "Who said I'm worried?"

"Lu."

"He was specific. The time. The place where he wants me to call him from."

"He's done that before."

She shrugged again and picked up her chopsticks. I offered her the carton, and she plucked out a thin strip of chicken.

"But this time feels different?" I asked.

"He wants to talk."

I waited. She didn't say anything more, so I fished through the other cartons on the side table, looking for something with vegetables. Found chow mein. Good enough. I scooped, chewed, swallowed.

"When was the last time you sent him a find?" I asked.

"Find" was a polite term for what most people would assume was a rusty piece of junk.

But that rust hid magical items that the reclusive collector had bought without fail for over forty years now.

We'd never met Headwaters. The few times Lu had been instructed to speak with the collector, a representative handled the call.

"Six months ago," she finally said. "That porcelain doll hand."

"Creepy doll hand that summons demons?"

"We don't know that's what it does."

"It's a disembodied doll hand. What else would it do?"

"I think it blesses water."

"Definitely summons demons."

"Just because it's magical doesn't mean it's evil."

"So it summons nice demons?"

She squinted at me and stole a piece of broccoli out of my container. I left it tipped her way, hoping she would eat more. She had always been slender, but since the attack that had left her half-vampire, she was downright lean.

"I don't have a find on me," she said. She picked a carrot from the box, glared at it, then dropped it in her mouth. "The closest storage unit is Tulsa. We could stop there before going to Arcadia to call Headwaters."

I paused with a clump of bean sprouts halfway to my mouth. "Pops is there."

"Who?"

"Where. The store and gas station. Pops."

"You want a Moxie Cola?"

"No. Well, yes, now that you bring it up, but that's where the seer—the owl woman—wanted me to meet her."

"You didn't tell me that. You just said in Arcadia. She was specific about that place?"

"In both visions."

"Maybe she's Headwaters," Abbi said.

"Why would you think that?" Lu asked.

"Brogan said some people aren't what they look like. Maybe she's not a seer. Maybe she's a trickster. Maybe she's whatever a Headwaters is."

I chewed and thought that over. It made some sense. Headwaters had been gathering magical items for almost half a century. He or she might be able to create visions with some of those items. But why contact me via a vision when calling Lu was easier and more straightforward?

"Brogan?" Lula asked.

I hummed. "I don't think so. Visions take a lot of energy, a lot of work. Headwaters texts and uses representatives to remain anonymous. But two people pushing us toward the same place is suspicious."

"We could refuse," Lu said. "We don't need the money and we don't owe Headwaters anything."

I set the carton down, my appetite sated for now. "We don't owe the owl woman anything, either."

"We could turn around," Lu said. "Stay with Ricky at the Crossroads? Visit Valentine? Been awhile since he's called. I'm sure he'd be happy to see you."

"Damn ghost," I said.

"Moon balls?" Abbi asked. "Can we make cookies? I mean, can we visit? I bet Ricky is super lonely for us."

"She's not lonely," I said. "She has that annoying werewolf ghost to keep her company."

Lu shook her head. "You like Valentine."

"He's a ghost. I very much do not like him. Besides, Cupid wants us looking for that book."

"Cupid hasn't told us there's a deadline," Lu said. "For all we know, the god's lost spell book is back in Missouri."

"Nope," Abbi said.

"Or Illinois," Lu said.

"Nope." Abbi pulled Hado onto her lap and petted his head. "I can hear it. It's not behind us. It's somewhere ahead."

"Ahead?" I asked.

"West, mostly." She petted Hado with strokes that were a little too determined.

"Abs," I said gently. I nodded toward her hand.

She blinked, as if coming back from wherever it was the book was calling, and gave me a half smile. "I like that. Abs." She rested her hand on Hado's back

"How far ahead of us is the book?" I asked.

She cocked her head to one side. "I can't tell. It's…
hard to hear, but it's west. I know it."

She started petting again, softer and slower. Hado
closed his eyes and purred.

"Made you purr," she told him.

He opened his moonstone eyes and yowled.

Abbi giggled and started petting him again. "Made
you purr. Just like a cat. A pretty, pretty cat. Are you a
pretty kitty, Hado? Pretty little fur ball?"

Hado put up an effort not to close his eyes and melt
into her soothing touch, but his lids closed once, twice,
and on the third time, the purring started up again.

Abbi slapped her free hand over her mouth, eyes
filled with delight.

"It feels like a trap," Lu said. "Going where Headwaters and your vision woman want us to go."

"Oh, it's undoubtedly a trap." I shoved at the
blanket with my feet, pushing until I could pull them up
over my hips. Not as easy as it seemed, since Lu and
Lorde were both on the outside of the covers. "We have
lots of things in the Tulsa storage, though."

"And?"

"We have plenty of minor magical doo-dads we can
give Headwaters. And plenty of weapons we can arm
ourselves with."

"Hold on, let me picture this," Lula said. "You,
striding into a soda shop wearing a sword, maybe mace
and chain, and an axe. Is that what you want us to do?"
The smile was back, along with the twinkle in her eye.

"Absolutely, that's what I want us to do."

"We'll get arrested."

"I want a sword too," Abbi said.

"No sword," both Lu and I said at the same time.

"But swords are cool," she muttered.

"We'll buy you cookies," I said, without looking away from Lu. "Because Lu and I will have the weapons. Lots of weapons. All the weapons. We'll protect you."

"And Hado," Abbi said.

"And we'll protect Hado."

The purr turned into a growl a cat should not make.

Lorde lifted her head, her pointed ears flopping, and tapped her tail a couple times.

"Hado will protect *us*," Abbi said. "Won't you, little kitty witty? Sweet fluffy purr-purr. So strong and fierce."

Hado tried to keep up the growl, but Abbi's petting was too soothing. He twisted onto his back, yawned, and went back to purring.

"No swords." Lu stood and shucked out of her jeans, then walked off toward the bathroom.

"Ugn…" I had to swallow to keep from choking on my own spit. "What?"

She paused in the bathroom doorway and tried to look stern, but I could see she was pleased. "No swords in the soda shop."

"Is this where we make a bet that one of us, and by one I mean me, is going to smuggle weapons into the soda shop?"

"No weapons and no bets you can't win."

"I always win."

She rolled her eyes, then shut the door.

"I win," I grumbled. "I win a lot."

Abbi covered her mouth again, trying to make very serious eyes as she nodded at me.

The shower turned on. The curtain clicked as rings pulled to one side, and the interrupted rhythm of the water filtered through the thin door as Lu ducked under the spray.

"You should take a sword." Abbi flopped back on the bed, then seemed to realize there was a blanket she could crawl under, and got busy burying herself, piling the four flat pillows over her head like layers of bread.

"Why do you think I need a sword?" I got up and took care of the empty food cartons, shoving them inside each other, then tying them in the bag and dropping them next to the tiny wastepaper basket so we could throw them away in the morning.

Her voice was muffled as she replied: "In case something bad happens."

"Do you think something bad's going to happen?"

The water shut off. Lu could probably hear both of us through the door.

"Something bad always happens," Abbi said.

"Maybe not always." Lu had stolen one of my T-shirts and was using it as a nightgown. It came to just above her knees. She was braiding her wet hair over one shoulder, her eyes absolutely luminous in the low light. "Sometimes good things happen."

"Yeah," I said, moving the covers aside and negotiating foot room with Lorde, "sometimes."

Lu padded to the door and switched off the light.

"But sometimes," I said, as my wife turned and glided my way, as she kneeled on the bed beside me, and settled her body next to mine, as familiar as my own breath. "Sometimes only the best things happen."

Lu pressed her palm against my chest, over my heart. I rested my hand over the back of hers and counted my exhales until I was gone.

CHAPTER FIVE

"It's wet," Abbi noted.

The windshield wipers on the old truck were going hard and losing ground to the flash flood that had opened over our head a second after Lu had gotten a weather warning on her phone.

Rain rattled against the metal roof and hood of the truck, like some shitty weather deity throwing buckets of gravel at us. I was starting to think even Lu's good eyesight wasn't going to be enough to keep us on the narrow, twisting road.

"Really wet," Abbi added. She was sitting between Lu and me, her legs crisscrossed, and was holding Hado against her chest like he could keep her dry.

"Rain's rain," I said. "It'll pass."

"The road is a river now."

I nodded. "Lu will pull over before it gets too bad. Maybe at the next pull out on higher ground?"

Lu looked relaxed behind the wheel, one hand on the top of it, the other resting on her thigh, but she was tense. "I can," she agreed, "but the storage isn't too much farther. We should just drive through and shelter there."

The sky flickered and thunder rolled like a celestial bass drum. Gravel turned into rocks, hammering away any answer I might have had.

Abbi squished in on herself, then turned to me and wedged behind my side, pulling my arm in front of her and holding on.

I patted whatever part of her was near my palm—her knee—and kept my eye on the road.

The flash flood dragged dirt off the hillside, blood red rivulets running onto the road, rusting and staining the water. Lu scowled through the next corner, the visibility even worse.

The water was rising. I yelled that we needed higher ground, a place to stop, but the racket swallowed my words.

We skidded up out of the gully we'd been in and took another corner slower than the last. Lu, her knuckles white on the wheel, had to be guessing where the road was.

The sky flashed, blinding, and Lu gestured, shouting, but I couldn't hear a word over the explosion of thunder that broke the world in half.

Abbi yanked on my arm. Lorde jumped down to the floor near my feet, which was why I was looking down.

Lu yelled, a furious curse-laden warning.

I jerked my head up—

—In time to see the headlights aiming straight at us—

—Abbi shrieked, Hado writhed and shifted—

—Lu was still swearing, her lip curled in a snarl as she yanked the wheel trying to force four thousand pounds of steel to do the impossible and avoid impact—

I braced my feet, trying to grab for Lorde, and hold Abbi in place, as the headlights swerved, but not fast enough, not far enough.

The world slapped us sideways. My head bounced off the window, pain sliced through my legs. Metal screamed. Sky, trees, water rolled around us like dirty laundry in a coin wash. A flash of sand-colored eyes, sharp teeth, and a woman's foot crushing my face, her strange laughter joyous and horrifying.

Then everything stopped.

I couldn't breathe. Water covered my head. I was drowning.

I thrashed, frantic with panic, while a wry voice in my head noted I was right about this old truck being the death of us.

Abbi pushed—no, pulled. I thought she was behind me, but she was in front, tugging at my shirt. I got my eyes open. My lungs burned. Air, I needed air.

It was too dark, the lightning and flash in the sky snuffed out by rain. Water everywhere, swamping my vision, stinging and blurring the world. Two hands yanked hard and dragged me out from beneath the water.

One piercing tone gonged loudly in my ears, making other sounds wooly and garbled beneath it. My stomach churned and I puked gallons of tepid water down the front of me.

I tried to brace my foot and howled as pain shot up my leg.

That pain cleared my head.

I could see.

It hadn't been Abbi trying to pull me out of the truck; it had been Lu. She was sopping wet, a trickle of blood painted through her hair, running red threads down her pale, pale face.

"…move," she yelled, "…truck…explode."

Finally, one sound—fire—chewed its way through my addled brain. "Where's…" I coughed, almost puked again, my head swimming and sick, then tried again. "Abbi? Lorde?"

Lu had me propped against her, my arm over her shoulder. The world bucked and swayed and I breathed through my mouth to keep my stomach stable. "Here," Lu said. "Over here. Abbi's hurt."

We waded through the river, my ankle giving me hell, then hell and a half as we climbed the berm to the road, where water flowed, ankle deep.

The storm had shifted from a downpour to a hard rain. Lighting strobed, throwing the trees, vines, and undergrowth beside the road into mercury-bright relief. Thunder crackled and snarled.

Lu shuffled me to the other side of the road and kept us moving until the truck, which had landed upside down, the smoldering engine fire already extinguishing, was yards behind us.

Hado came into view first. He stood with shoulders hunched, arms drawn toward his chest to cradle something small as if he were trying to keep it dry.

Lorde stood facing us, her tail up, her mouth open and panting in worry, but otherwise looking unharmed.

Where was Abbi?

Hado shifted slightly, and I saw what he held. It was a tiny gray bunny. But instead of resting with legs curled up under it, the bunny sprawled on its side, limp in his arms, eyes closed, and breath coming too quickly.

Blood matted her fur.

"Abbi," I breathed. "Is she..." Lorde moved up beside me and paced a full circle around Lu and me, making little whining noises. I dropped my free hand and rubbed at her head. She leaned into my leg. "How badly is Abbi hurt?" I asked.

Hado wasn't much of a talker. The very few times I had heard him speak, his words had formed more in my head than in my ears. This time was no different.

"She needs a healer."

"We can't use the truck," Lu said. "Your phone is broken. One of us needs to take Abbi and go for help."

"I can—"

"You can't," Lu cut off my suggestion. "Your ankle won't let you. It has to be me or Hado. I'm very fast and pass as human better than Hado does."

"You're bleeding," I said.

Hado scowled and pulled Abbi closer to his chest.

"It has to be me," Lu said. "I can find a hospital, I can talk to people, pay them money. I can find a doctor or...or a vet."

"Healer," Hado said again. *"Not a doctor."*

"Doctor is the best we'll find." Lu reached for Abbi.

"I'll take her with me. I'll take care of her, Hado. You protect Brogan until I can get a car here to you."

"I don't need protecting, and you're bleeding," I argued. "No," I said to her glare, "I'm not saying you shouldn't run Abbi into the nearest town, but you don't go alone. Take Hado. Lorde and I will stay here and recover what we can from the truck."

Lu narrowed her eyes. "Absolutely not. I'm not leaving you stranded alone in the rain."

"Rain ain't gonna last forever. We'll be fine." Despite my best effort, a shiver rattled me head to heel. Shock, I supposed, from banging my head and almost drowning.

Lu shook her head and winced from the movement. "I won't—"

Lorde barked and trotted into the road, headed back to the truck.

"Lorde!" I shouted.

"Come," Lu said at the same time.

Lorde stopped right in the damn middle of the road and wagged her tail.

A van was headed toward us, high beams on, driving slow, and slower once it came alongside the truck in the ditch.

Lu jogged off to get Lorde, but the fool dog was still barking at the van, tail swishing. Lu hooked Lorde's collar and guided our fuzzy girl over to the shoulder next to us. The van moved forward, stopping next to her.

Hazard lights blinked gold in the gloom, and the driver's side window rolled down. "Are you Lula and Brogan Gauge?" a man called out.

No one should know who we were. No one should know where we were. No one should even be looking for us. But we didn't live a logical sort of life. There were all sorts of deities and creatures that might decide to track us, though I wouldn't have a clue as to their reason for doing so.

"Do you need help?" he asked. "A ride? A tow truck? I've got towels and blankets."

"Who are you?" Lu called back. "Who sent you?"

"Lawrence Hobbs. Miss Woodbury. She lives up aways and thought you might be in trouble, though she said I'd find you a few miles back. Good thing I kept going. But then, she's not always dead on in her prognostications. But she said you might need a healer, and well, I'm the best we've got around here."

"Woodbury?" Lu asked.

"She said she sent her owls to talk to Mr. Gauge. Does she have that wrong too?"

"The seer," I said, unnecessarily, from the look Lu gave me. Yeah, the punch to the head was still making my thoughts muzzy. "It might be a trap."

Hado strode toward the van, determination in every step, and Lorde followed him.

"Fuck it," Lu said. "Can you walk?"

"I'm fine." My teeth chattered the words, but she didn't call me on my lie. She slipped her arm around my waist and helped me across the road.

Lorde wagged her tail harder as we approached, then wove around to walk on my other side toward the van.

"Pretty sure this is how psychotic murderers lure in their victims," I said.

"Lot of work to go out in a flash flood just for a little killing," she noted.

"Let's hope so. You have your knives?"

"Always."

"Good," I said.

She squeezed my side, then we were at the driver's side door, and the man was smiling at us.

He was bald, dark-skinned, with an impressive thick, dark beard, a wide face, and black-rimmed glasses. "I promise I'm not an axe murderer."

"Which is exactly what an axe murderer would say," I said.

His smile grew. "That's the problem, isn't it? They know how to pass as helpers. But I think you'd know, both of you would know, if I were out here for evil doings. I'm hoping one of you is in good enough shape to drive, so I can take a look at the little rabbit. She's not a rabbit, is she?"

So that put some questions to rest. He was obviously aware of the otherness of the world, the strange and supernatural. It made believing he was sent by the seer —Miss Woodbury—that much easier.

"I can drive," Lu said. "His foot is injured."

"Bring him on around." He opened the door, unbuckled his seatbelt, then twisted and squeezed between the van seats and into the back of the vehicle.

Lu started walking with me toward the passenger side, but I lifted my arm off her shoulder and deposited a kiss near her temple. "I got this. Go ahead and get behind the wheel."

Thunder bowled overhead, hitting three strikes in a row, and Lu must have agreed there was an advantage to her being in control of the vehicle. She released her hold and slipped into the driver's seat. I kept one hand on the van and hobbled my way to the door, Lorde still at my side.

I pushed up into the warm interior. Lorde did us all a favor and shook off an Olympic swimming pool worth of rain before jumping up after me.

I shut the door and assessed what we'd just gotten ourselves into.

Trees, fern, moss, mushrooms covered the walls and space where another set of benches might usually be. For a moment, I thought I'd stumbled out of the van and somehow landed in a rainforest. But then I noticed the mesh wire racks on the walls into which the pots and containers were hooked.

"I teach classes," Lawrence Hobbs said, answering my unspoken question. He gently ran his fingers over the bunny, who was still deathly still and bleeding in Hado's arms. "This is my mobile classroom. I go into urban areas and show kids how to get their hands into the soil and make green things grow. Explain water cycles, growing cycles, our natural world."

He glanced at me. "Usually, I have a lot more razzmatazz in here, but I'm waiting for some sprouts to root before I start the classroom tour circuit."

"You said you were a healer," I said.

"I am. Or as close to one as can be found around

here. But my day job is being Mother Nature's roadie." He smiled, and his glasses shifted upward on his cheeks. "Go on and ask the questions you want to ask, but Lula? If you could head us toward Tulsa, that'd be great. I have a place there you can stay for the night."

"A murder hotel?" I asked.

Another smile tugged his lips, but his attention was on Abbi, assessing her injuries. I had the feeling he could see more of her than just the bunny she appeared to be.

"Friends of mine are out of town—at their daughter's wedding. They said I could use their place any time. Seems like now is a pretty good time."

Lu didn't ask for directions. There was only this one road, and she probably knew how to get to Tulsa better than the residents. The van handled the road well enough. The plants should make the space feel closed in and musty, instead it felt comfortable and safe. Lorde had already found a spot of floor to curl up and was softly snoring.

"Can you turn her over?" Lawrence asked Hado. "Or…" He reached into the greenery and magically conjured a small table with a soft pillow topper that could easily double for a bed. "Would you feel comfortable enough to lay her here?"

Hado didn't even hesitate. He very carefully and gently settled Abbi onto the pillow.

Lawrence was silent and attentive, his fingers quick and efficient. "You were all in the accident? In that truck in the ditch?"

"Yes," I said.

"Could you tell what spell hit you?"

"That's not…"

—sand-colored eyes, sharp teeth, and a woman's foot crushing my face, her strange laughter joyous and horrifying—

I looked over at Lu. She was frowning, lines between her eyebrows.

"I don't think magic was involved." Doubt softened my statement.

"It was magic. Or if not that," Lawrence reached overhead and produced a handful of tiny daisy-like flowers that had not been there a moment before, "it was some kind of power. This wound isn't as deep as it looks," he told Hado. "I assume you can tell she's not mortally wounded?"

Hado paused. His scowl didn't waver, but he gave one curt nod.

"And you may also know that this wound is both strange and very serious. Inflicted by magic."

—a woman. Why had I seen a woman in the crash—

"Power," Hado agreed.

The van took a corner, and I braced my hand on the wall next to me. Moss compressed under my palm, cool and soft between my fingers. A soothing wash of comfort flooded through me like I'd just had a massage or a pint of beer. A soft piping song I could barely hear asked a question, invited a conversation.

An answering hum from the mushrooms on the other side of the van rolled through me. I lifted my hand away from the moss and the songs and humming ended.

Hado didn't seem to be paying any attention to me. Lu's eyes were on the road, and Lawrence was adding leaves to a small cup of water, whispering as he did so.

He wasn't a witch. I knew witches.

He wasn't a god. I knew gods.

But I didn't think he was a healer, exactly, either.

Every green thing in the van responded to him. They leaned toward him as he whispered, as if each syllable was light and water.

Fae? Druid?

"Druid," he said, answering my unspoken question. "As I said, as close to a healer in these parts as would find you quick enough. This will help, but it won't remove the magical impact of the wound. We'll need something more focused on breaking that kind of thing. None of the plants here can do that."

"Why can't they?" I asked.

"Like I said, I teach classes. How to dig in the dirt, how to replant, how to know if a plant has enough water. Magic, other than a bit of focus and care, is not required for these greens." He tipped a water bottle onto a thick cotton pad and then positioned the pad, along with the leaves and other bits of twig and seed, onto Abbi's side, over her wound.

Hado's nostrils flared, but he didn't slap away the compress or try to kill Lawrence, so whatever the druid was doing wasn't harmful.

The van took another wide corner, and the road beneath the tires changed, the sound quieter and lower. We'd come out of the storm, or more likely, the storm had moved on past us.

Lawrence swept his fingers across the floor and there were three polished pebbles in his hand. Rose quartz, obsidian, and red jasper. He placed the quartz on Abbi's head and offered Hado the obsidian. Hado took the stone without a question. Lawrence kept the jasper and brought it up to his heart, holding it there.

"Rest, little spirit," he whispered. "All life is here to nurture you. This Earth your mother, this Earth your home."

The rabbit took a deeper breath, and her ears twitched. Then her breathing settled, falling into rhythm with Lawrence's breathing, and, if I listened closely, with that green unsung song that surrounded us.

"This won't be enough to heal her fully," Lawrence said. "You'll need a real healer or a healing spell for her to recover, and you'll need it soon. And since I'm giving advice, you aren't in very good shape yourself."

"I'm fine," I said.

"For someone with a concussion and sprained ankle, maybe. Lula also needs care."

"I don't," she snapped.

He spread his hands. "I see that you share a stubbornness. Good. You'll need it, I'm sure."

"Why will we need it?"

"Miss Woodbury doesn't tell me to go scoop two people, a shadow, a rabbit, and a dog off the road in the middle of a flash flood every day. If it's important enough for her to step in, it involves more than the natural world. And if you need my help—her help— then you are mixed up in things much stranger than the common traveler faces."

"Can you help Lu?" I asked.

"Still fine," she said, not taking her attention off the road.

But she wasn't. I wasn't fine either. We both knew it and didn't want to admit it. One of us had to be smart about this.

"All right," I sighed. "Do you know a doctor?" I could feel Lu's gaze on me, her displeasure that I'd accepted we both needed medical attention.

"I have a friend down at the clinic who can look at you. He'd be a good with…well, with what Lula needs too."

There was something cagey about the way he said that. How he wasn't giving name to her injuries. My reactions, my thinking, were sluggish, but worry was crawling its way through the fog in my head. If this stranger could see it, how badly was she hurt?

"But as I said, you'll need to get stronger healing for the rabbit. Soon."

"We have what she needs," Lu said.

"A healer?" he asked.

"A healing shroud."

His dark eyebrows ticked up. "That's rare. But good. Yes, if it's strong—"

"It's strong."

"Then it should break the magic that's holding her. Is it nearby?"

"A few miles."

His whole face lit up. "Good. Yes, good. The compress will last a few miles for sure." He shifted his hand with the rock, which was still resting against his chest, pressing it closer over his heart, lending his strength to help Abbi.

"So." He leaned back against the wall opposite me,

his free hand in the fronds of a sword fern, his sneak-ered feet flat on the floor, knees bent. "You had questions. What do you want to know?"

"Tell me about Miss Woodbury," I said. "Have you met her?"

"Yes."

"Is she a seer?"

"Yes. As much as."

"What does that mean?"

"Not everything fits neatly in a box. People, abilities, assumptions. It's hard to put one name to Miss Woodbury. She sees things. Much of it is accurate. She… influences things. But she doesn't know everything. Free will always throws a wrench into the cosmic machinery."

"What does she want with us?"

"I have no idea. She called me, told me to look for Lula and Brogan Gauge, told me where you'd be."

"So you just drop everything and do what she tells you?" The van hit a hard patch of road and a headache rattled through my skull.

"She's a friend. She's done favors for me in the past, so I do favors for her. You're a very suspicious man for someone who's just been rescued from a rollover in the middle of a flash flood."

"All the more reason to be suspicious." I rubbed at my forehead. Didn't ease the headache.

"What threw you into the ditch? Bad tires?"

"Avoiding a front-end collision with a car headed straight at us."

"You must have been off the road for quite a while."

"You showed up less than five minutes after we were run off the road," Lu said.

The lines around his mouth dug in as his lips pulled down. "That can't be right. I didn't see a car pass me. There aren't any side roads, houses, or pullouts. If someone had run you off the road, I would have seen them."

The van hit another bump, and I pressed my hand over my eyes to keep my brains from falling out.

"You missed them," I said.

"No…" He shifted and tapped my arm.

I dropped my hand and squinted at him. He pressed another soft cloth, this one filled with something that smelled of peppermint and rosemary, against my eyes. The relief was immense. I took over, holding it over my aching head.

"I couldn't have missed someone on the road," he said.

"Swell. I saw the car…"

—*sandpaper eyes, unhinged laughter delighting in our pain*—

"…Lu saw the car. We wouldn't have landed in the ditch if there hadn't been a car."

"The car was real," Lu's voice hinged, tight. She was angry, worried. I should do something about both those things, but the pounding in my head was chewing up my attention.

"If it *wasn't* a car," Lawrence went on, "it could have been something else. Illusion? Trick of light?"

"Nightmare," I mumbled.

"Power," Hado said, or maybe said again.

"Same thing," I said. "Magic. Power. Power. Magic."

Hado grunted, which I took as a disagreement. Abbi made a small, wounded sound.

I pulled the compress off my eyes. Both Hado and Lawrence were working over the small bunny, checking her head and neck and legs.

She made more small, pitiful sounds.

"What does she need?" I asked. "What can we do?"

"We can drive faster," Lawrence said.

The van lurched, and Lu drove faster.

RAIN BECAME A DRONING DRIZZLE, just enough to make standing out in it for any length of time uncomfortable.

I didn't like bringing a stranger to one of our storage units, but we needed the vehicle, and neither Lu nor I wanted to stop long enough to kick Lawrence out.

Abbi had been whining in pain for the last mile, and Hado had only become angrier and more protective.

I was worried he was going to pick her up and make a run for it, but Lawrence somehow managed to both change Abbi's compress and keep Hado calm enough that the shadow hadn't made a break for it yet.

Lu slowed the van, taking the speed bumps hard. I grunted at the spike of pain in my skull and spine, and swallowed to keep from getting sick all over the potted plants.

Lawrence's hand rested on Abbi's hip. Without looking my way, he offered me a sprig of something yellow. "Chew. It will help."

The sweet peppery scent of ginger hit my nostrils. I

took the root from him and bit down on it, holding it between my molars.

My stomach lurched with the van over the next two speed bumps, and then Lu put the van into park and pushed out the door, running into the cold and drizzle.

It had been years since we'd been here, at least a decade, but Lu never forgot codes or locks. Lu never lost keys.

She jogged back, got behind the wheel, and was driving before she'd even closed the door. We rumbled through the gate, past several squat, square metal buildings with formidable brown bay doors.

I smelled smoke a moment before Lu tapped the brakes. "Shit!" She threw the van into park and bolted out the door.

Our storage unit was at the end of a row of twenty other units.

It was also on fire.

CHAPTER SIX

The van door hammered against the stops and slapped back, clipping my shoulder as I shot out after Lula. My bad foot hit the concrete. I howled, but kept going.

Smoke, slow and thick, bellowed out of the storage unit. The bay door had lost a bracket and hung like a broken sail over the gap, fire licking across the frame. Beyond it was more smoke, more fire, and Lula running into the building.

"Lula! No." I jogged through the door, my ankle screaming with pain. Hot, acid air burned my lungs and set off new layers of lightning-strike agony in my head, silver in the darkness of my brain, blinding.

I stopped, retched, hands on knees, my entire body shaking, before I pushed forward, stumbling. The right wall. I wouldn't get lost if I followed the wall.

I plunged into the dark smoke and hit my shoulder on something solid—a shelf. Metal and glass shattered on the floor. I threw my arm over my mouth, trying to breathe.

Visibility narrowed down and down. Glimpses of Lula, her hair, flashes of her pale skin blurred with another woman's face. A woman with sharpened teeth danced beside me, sandpaper eyes, her laughter fuel to the fire, cruel and delighted.

The storage room became a tunnel, and that tunnel closed in on me, humming, ringing, the sounds growing softer.

The woman's voice crooned in my ear. "Die old mortal, die new flesh. Your bones will be my key."

A string of popping explosions rang out from the far side of the building, like someone had set off fireworks.

Where was Lula?

There should be sprinklers on the ceiling. There should be a fire department. There should be alarms.

Unless this was planned.

Unless this was sparked by magic—

—"*Your bones will be my key.*"—

Unless this was a trap, one Lu had charged headlong into without even a backward glance.

I was really reeling now, walls of smoke pressing in, the light at the end of that long, long tunnel fading.

My feet moved, but I couldn't feel them anymore, not even the pain in my ankle. The world herked and jerked and something clipped my knees. I folded like a wet rag.

A strong hand caught my elbow. I couldn't see who it was, because I couldn't see.

"Here. Now." The voice was a growl—Hado.

Lu. Where was Lu?

I pulled against Hado's grip, but the smoke had done its job on me and Hado was strong. He forced me to the left, and then, when I thought he was taking us even further into the burning building, there was a square of light ahead that grew larger and larger.

Just before I staggered out of the storage unit, the sprinklers kicked on, water rushing from above.

I tried to fight my way free, but Hado tightened his grip. I was forced by the moon's shadow, away from the flames, away from the smoke, away from the building, away from Lu.

"Lu," I gasped, with what little air I had. I coughed until I couldn't breathe. "Lu's. In. There."

Hado steered me mercilessly to the van.

Lawrence trotted over, and between the two of them, they got me where they wanted. Lawrence handed me a wet washcloth. "Over your mouth. It will help."

I slapped it over my mouth and pivoted to get back to the unit. "Lu."

"Here," she said, behind me.

My heart flopped and relief hit me so hard, that if Hado wasn't still holding my arm, I'd have been on the ground.

I reached for her and she stepped into me, her arms going around my waist. Her face was covered in dirt, or maybe just soot. She held on tight. I didn't know which of us was shivering.

"I thought…" Those two words were enough to rust

up my lungs. I sipped air to oil them but that set off another harsh coughing fit.

"I'm okay," she said, rubbing my back. "You shouldn't have gone in there, Brogan. Shouldn't have come after me."

"You—"

"I'm fast. A hell of a lot faster than you. I was in and out of the building almost before you got there."

It wasn't often I underestimated my wife, but, well, today was one of those times.

"Never," she warned, "do that again."

She dragged her hand up and pressed it over my heart. "Never." It was a threat.

"I'd promise," I wheezed, "but I don't lie to you, love."

She scowled at me, but it only lasted a second. Then she pointed at the van's open rear doors. "Let Lawrence heal you."

"Still not a healer," Lawrence said. At Lu's look, he quickly added, "Yep, let me take a look and then we'll get you both to a doctor."

The adrenalin I'd been running on washed out of me like water down a drain. My headache was off the charts and other aches were making themselves known.

I moved my ass and sat in the back of the van. I might have closed my eyes while Lawrence gently checked my scalp, neck, shoulders, arms, chest.

I was going to ask about Abbi, was going to ask how Lu had talked Hado into leaving her to go after me, but Lawrence tipped a cup of water to my lips and the water was so good, it became my world.

"…doing better," Lawrence said. I blinked and pushed my head and shoulders off the van wall where I'd been leaning.

"I think the shroud was enough, but again, not a healer. Now that she's stabilized, I'm going to take you and Brogan to a doctor."

"We can't," Lula said.

"Someone's going to notice that fire," he said, like they'd already done a lap or two on this subject and weren't anywhere closer to the finish line. "We don't want to be here when they do."

"I'll make sure no one sees it." Lu might have gotten in and out of the fire fast, but her voice was lower, roughened by smoke.

"Magic?" he asked.

"Not everything was damaged. Most of it survived. I'll need to get a few things to cast the illusion."

"How long will the illusion last?"

"A few days. Long enough."

"Long enough for what?"

"For me to get everything in there somewhere else."

I cleared my throat. "Without a truck?"

She was next to me then, and I couldn't help but open my eyes to see her.

Gods, she was beautiful. She had wiped most of the ash off her face, but a thin line of it framed her hairline, the corners of her eyes, and darkened her eyebrows.

"Hey, you awake again?"

"Just resting my eyes," I grumbled, which pulled a smile out of her. "Is Abbi okay?"

"She's doing better. Just behind you there."

Hado sat inside on the floor, his back against the van wall. Abbi, the girl, not the rabbit, was curled up on his lap, wrapped in a soft old magical Pendleton blanket. She held the rose quartz in her hand, and I swear it glowed pink.

Hado's eyes were the cool luminous gray of burnished pewter. I nodded at him in thanks for saving my life. He nodded back in thanks for saving Abbi's.

"Always did like that old blanket," I said.

Lu handed me a cup of water, and I squinted at it suspiciously. "Last time I drank something, I fell asleep."

"It's just water. How's your head?"

"Peachy," I lied. Then, because I wasn't that much of an ass: "I need a doctor, or so the druid says."

Lu nodded. "You do. We'll find his friend's clinic. I need to throw an illusion on the storage unit."

"We. We need to throw an illusion. I'm coming with you."

Emotions duked it out across her face, and I saw the winners. She was going to refuse my help.

"You're strong," I said. "Incredibly strong. Physically, mentally. Your heart." I had to smile. "So strong. But magic? Lu, you know magic is always better when we use it together. It always has been."

That set off another war, and I wasn't sure which emotion would win this time.

"Ghosts," I said, making my case. "Stella from back in McLean. You couldn't see her, talk to her, but I could. But you were the one who could let her step into your body so she could talk to her sister, Dot. And I was the one who could de-possess her out of you. Magic, any of it, works better when we both have our hands on it."

"I could have—"

"Handled Stella? Yes, you could have. You would have figured something out. But together, we are stronger. After all these years, I know that. We know that. We make a hell of a team. Especially with magic. Let's make this as fast and easy as possible before my headache makes me black out."

That did it. Battle won.

"You're slurring your words." She moved so I could get out of the vehicle.

"That's the concussion speaking." I was careful not to move my head too quickly, and as long as I didn't breathe too deeply, or put much weight on my left foot, well, I was just aces.

Lu had already catalogued my injuries, but this gave me a chance to see hers. Her stride was shortened, her shoulders slightly hunched, and she kept one arm across her stomach. She was hurting, too.

As soon as we were out of ear-shot of the van, I caught her hand with my own. "Are you okay?"

She changed her stride to match my hobble as we approached the stinking, smoldering mess of a storage unit.

"Yes."

I stopped and when she took that extra step, I pulled her back to me so we were facing each other. "How badly are you hurt, love?"

Her mouth drew straight and her teeth pressed small indents into the soft flesh of her lips. I squeezed her hand gently. "We're a team," I coaxed. "You know I have a concussion, twisted ankle, and my lungs are shit for air. Tell me where you're hurting."

She touched the top of her head. "A cut, I think, from the accident. Not bad. My ribs are bruised. I don't think they're broken."

She was telling the truth, but there was something more she wasn't saying. Something Lawrence had hinted at when he'd said she needed care.

"And the rest? What aren't you telling me?"

"We need to choose a find out of the unit for Headwaters. We need to cast the illusion before the local fire department shows up."

I stepped into her, close enough her pupils grew wide and dark. She swayed toward me, then shivered as if I were a fire, and she was snow-blind and lost. "What else, love?" I asked softer, lower, though the smoke had wrecked my vocal chords.

"I'm not…." She swallowed, her gaze focused on the side of my neck, her breathing gone choppy.

"Lula."

She licked her lips and leaned back, her chin up, gaze very obviously not on my neck. "I'm hungry." It was an admission of failure. An apology. "Not for food," she added stiffly.

I blamed my rattled brains for not picking up on it earlier. "You need blood?"

Lula had been attacked by a vampire, or a monster close enough to one that it had left her in a half-state. She wasn't quite human, nor was she a vampire. She didn't need to eat much food on a regular basis, nor sleep as much as a human.

Blood alone wasn't enough for her survival either, but every so often, she needed blood. When that happened, she'd usually do something like steal a chicken from someone's farm. More rarely, she'd need more blood than a bird could offer.

"But I'm fine. It's just…you're hurt. Abbi. And Lawrence is… It's nothing I can't handle."

"Breathe," I said. "We have time."

She glanced over at the unit, then closed her golden eyes. She inhaled, exhaled, both slowly. After a few breaths, her shoulders softened, and she nodded. "I'm okay." She opened her eyes, and the sun rose in them. "Let's get the item, the illusion, and get out of here."

The fire was down to the occasional flame, ceiling sprinklers having drowned out the worst of it. The stink of wet charred wood and metal and other fried material was overwhelming. I had to take shallow breaths through my mouth to keep from choking on it.

"I don't know what kind of illusion is gonna hide this mess," I said.

Lu squinted at the darkness. Something inside fell and landed with a wet plop. "I think we have the wool carder and spindle in there."

"Not sure we have time to weave a rug."

She gave a quick shake of her head. "We should be able to pull a thread or two over the doorway and make it seem like nothing happened."

"Literally pulling the wool over their eyes? How is that even a real spell?"

Her smile was small, but real. "All the old sayings and rhymes were about magic. You know that."

I did know that, but it was good to make her smile.

She poked a finger into my chest. "Stay out here. This will only take me a few seconds."

"No."

"Brogan. Your head. Your lungs. Your ankle."

"All of them good enough for me to not let my wife go alone into a dangerous, burned storage room filled with powerful, and possibly damaged or compromised magical items."

"Faster," she jerked a thumb toward her chest. "Breathe less, better night vision."

A helicopter's blades thumped through the sky. Maybe coming this way, maybe not. But it put a point on us getting on with it.

"How about if I just come in a short distance? Just inside the doorway."

"If I'd known how bullheaded a man you were…" Lu started.

"You'd have married me sooner," I finished.

"Yes," she said, because this was a truth we never took for granted. "I would have."

I followed. The stink was ten times worse inside the unit.

I put my arm over my mouth, and Lu pointed to the back left corner of the building. "That's where it used to be. I'll go that way and be right back."

She disappeared into the shadows and gloom. I waited a heartbeat, right inside the doorway as I'd promised, then I started off to the right. There were some very valuable things on this side of the unit. And one particular thing I wanted to see for myself.

It was dark, but my vision adjusted so long as I kept blinking to clear tears. The thump and scratching sounds of Lu dragging finds around, maybe even digging out the wool carder and spindle, filtered over the clicking and dripping of combustibles shedding ash and water.

I stepped over a burned out box of clothing, turned my shoulders sideways, and squeezed through the space between two shelves that had toppled in toward each other. I found what I wanted on the other side of those shelves. Books.

Lu had boxes and totes of books. Each book had been wrapped carefully in paper, cloth, or that plastic bubble wrap. Not every book was magic. Some were rare editions, or oddities that she'd bought on a whim.

But most of the books contained spells, diagrams, and other arcane knowledge.

The intruder, because now I could say without a doubt there had been one—

—*sharp teeth and cardboard eyes, delight amidst the chaos*—

—had torn through the books like a two-bit bargain hunter at a rummage sale. Overturned totes sat on haphazard hills of books, cardboard boxes ripped open and shredded. More books had been scattered, thrown, and kicked.

Whatever the intruder wanted, they'd thought one of these books contained it. I couldn't tell which volume might be missing, nor if any actually were. But the charred pages and spines, and the melted remains of a gasoline can, told me this was where the fire had started.

That the books were still whole showed the strength of the magic that protected them. I stepped around the pile of books, reaching for the item I was looking for.

A plain silver letter opener with an ivory hilt, that despite its mundane design, nevertheless drew the eye to the mercury bright edge that was too sharp for something as fragile as paper.

I'd always known it was something more. Something legendary. Something deadly in the right hands.

Maybe even something deadly enough to kill the creature that hunted us.

I tucked it into my back pocket and turned.

"I saw this." Lu appeared at my side. I thought I'd have to explain why I wanted the letter opener, but her anger was aimed at the pile of books. "I don't know what they took."

"I'll give you a guess what they were looking for."

"The spell book of the gods," she said.

"Yep." We hadn't had anyone break into our storage before. Not before we'd run across that book and made our deal with Cupid.

She tugged on my elbow. "Let's go."

"Did you get something for Headwaters?"

She patted her front pocket. "Out."

It was hard to leave all the books in such a state, but we needed that illusion spell in place, fast. And no matter how much I tried to ignore the pain in my head and ankle, nothing had gotten better with me tromping around.

Outside, Lu handed me the carders—two square-headed wooden brushes with metal teeth that resembled dog brushes—and a bag of wool. She kept the spindle.

I positioned myself on one side of the door, and pulled out a handful of wool, brushing it in one direction through the carders.

The zing of magic coming off of the wool and carders slithered up my arm. Good.

I gave Lu the wool, and she worked it with the spindle, twisting it into fiber, whispering the words to a quirky old spell that sounded half ballad, half nursery rhyme as she walked backward toward the other side of the doorway. The string grew long between us, stretching and twisting, tiny sparks of blue and green magic snapping brightly, and winking away.

Lu was good at the mechanics and connections of spellwork. She'd always been quick to pick up languages and nuance, better than I at both. My wheelhouse was the visual side of things and the actual writing of spells. If a magic could be seen, I'd see it. If a god power could be spotted, I'd spot it. If a spell could be drawn to hold magic, I could draw it.

We'd fallen into those talents easily and never questioned it.

Lu finished the verse and gave me a nod. I placed the carder, with the wool bitten deep into in its teeth, onto the ground, then picked up the string Lu had spun, encouraging slack so I could loop it over the edge of the broken door, then down, hooking it into a ragged burr near the bottom of the door. Then I snagged the string of wool to the top edge of the frame around the open threshold.

Lu handed me the spindle, and let the thread slip between her fingers as she began the spell again. I retraced my steps, draping the wool in the places that were the most secure, a broken spider's web, creating an imperfect warp and weft as I went. Placing the thread was like drawing a spell, only my medium was magical wool, soaked through with Lula's words.

I tied the spindle and the carder fibers together, knotted the wool around both, and set them on the ground just inside the unit.

Lula was on the third pass of the spell. I stood behind her, my hands on her shoulders.

Her last syllable was short and high, a bird chirp that echoed back as if she had suddenly whistled in a cave.

Magic which had been sparking sleepily woke, stretched, and inched down the strings, scenting out the pattern I'd laid, and the intent Lu and I had both poured into the work.

It needed to look the same, smell the same as it did before the fire. It needed to look like all the other units around it.

It needed to draw no attention, turn away curious eyes, dampen clever ears.

Nothing happened.

My head throbbed with anvil strikes, a steady jack hammering pain.

But then…oh, but then.

The thread sparkled, like lightning bugs come alight

on the string. I held my breath, not wanting to miss a moment of this gentle magic.

In a blink, the sparkles lifted, a wave, a wash, a whirling ember-caught wind of firefly lanterns dancing and weaving in and out of my clumsily threaded tapestry, completing the lines in the negative space, until there was no burned out door, and no charred darkness beyond.

The smoke was gone; the air scented with the sweet warmth of cottonwood leaves in the sun.

The storage unit was whole again. Squat and beige, the brown door hung straight, rolled down into place with the same lock on it as every other unit.

The illusion was seamless, fed by the words of magic Lu had spoken and the flow of magic pouring up through the wool drawn spell.

Abbi had the healing blanket, the fire damage was hidden. We still needed the healer, but had time to take a moment to breathe.

"That," I said, drawing Lu's back against my chest, "was a damn fine sight of magic, Mrs. Gauge."

She melted into me, her body a line of entirely different fire.

"It's beautiful," she agreed.

"You make it look easy."

"So do you." She turned in my arms and held me briefly, her mouth near my heart. "They were after the book."

"I know."

"Why burn out the unit?"

"To hide any traces of their work?"

"To hide what they stole from us?" she countered. "There were so many rare artifacts in that unit, Brogan. So many things they could have taken."

"I know. Or this could have been a ruse. A…a trap."

She stilled. "To kill us?"

"Someone ran us off the road. Someone was in the unit when we got here."

"You saw someone?" She leaned back, her face tipped up, the gray light of the passing storm making her look like carved marble.

"A woman. I saw her eyes, her teeth. Heard her laughter."

"Who was she?"

"I don't know."

"What was she?"

I hesitated. Monster, god, fae, or immortal? "Power. She was power. Chaos. I can't…I can't remember her clearly. My head." I grunted, angry. "It's all a muddle right now. If she didn't find what she wanted…"

"We have other units. She'll target the other units."

"Unless she did find what she wanted."

"I can ask some people to check in on our storage units. Make some calls."

"I told you we should have left a crystal ball in each unit so we could spy on them all at once."

"I don't think it works that way."

"Jigger together a switchboard of Ouija boards?"

She quirked an eyebrow. "Are you teasing me, Brogan Gauge, or is this the concussion talking?"

"Just spit-balling ideas." I glanced at the unit. "That really is a fine thing. Good magic. Good work. "

She shifted so she could inspect it. "It's strange."

I hummed.

"It makes me happy. A burned out storage unit with a cheap wool illusion shouldn't make me this happy."

"Well, maybe it's not the storage unit and spell that is making you happy. Maybe it's something else. *Someone* else. I nominate me and second the nomination. I'm the thing that's making you happy."

She leaned into me again, her back to my chest. "This is the first time we've really used magic together now that you're…here with me. I liked you being a part of casting magic. I liked creating that focus of power with you."

"I've always been a part of the magic you've used, Lula. Even when you couldn't see me or feel me."

"I have always felt you." She paused, because we hadn't had time to talk this out, not really. We hadn't had time to tell each other how hard it had been, going near on a hundred years together, but without each other.

"I have always been there," I repeated. "Even when you decided to buy that creepy doll hand and sell it to Headwaters, claiming it was magic."

"It was magic." She turned out of my arms. "Just because you don't like a thing doesn't mean it isn't magic. Powerful magic."

"Sometimes a creepy doll hand is just a creepy doll hand," I noted.

We started toward the van, and I was still impressed by the complete lack of smoke in the air. If I put on my logical brain and did the math on how a real physical substance could be masked by a very unreal illusion, it made my head hurt more.

It took better souls than me to understand magic's inner gears and pulleys.

"You tuck another doll limb in your pocket for Headwaters? A foot? An elbow? Back of a knee?"

"The harmonica."

"What harmonica?"

"I picked it up in…must have been just outside Winslow. That farm house that had burned down. It was in the floorboards."

"Oh, you mean the *cursed* harmonica."

"It's not cursed."

"The house burned down to the studs, Lu."

"Bad wiring did that, not a harmonica."

"That's just what the harmonica wants you to think."

That pulled a short laugh out of her, and then we were at the van.

Lawrence, in the driver's seat, called out, "Get in. I'm going to feel a lot better once we get you two into a doctor."

At the sound of his voice, the reminder that there was a human druid near enough to bite, all the softness and ease went out of Lu, like someone had just welded her spine. I could almost feel the micro-adjustments in her, the changes she was making so that she wouldn't show what she was really feeling.

It wasn't anger. It was hunger.

The faster we saw a doctor and found some unsuspecting chickens, the better.

Lu motioned me toward the back while she took the front passenger seat.

I ducked into the verdant green of root and frond, and ignored the subtle song, something happy, something welcoming, as if a friend had returned. I settled in the back corner where I could keep an eye on Hado, the sleeping Abbi, and also Lula, and the druid who were both watching the road ahead.

The letter opener in my pocket was hard enough to be uncomfortable, so I shifted my hip. I wondered why Lu hadn't said anything about it. She had always treated it like it was much more dangerous than it seemed. Maybe she hadn't noticed I was carrying it. Or maybe she approved I did.

Abbi had told me to take a sword to the meeting with the seer, Miss Woodbury, and I wasn't fool enough to ignore that sort of advice.

"I'D LIKE YOU TO SIT." Dr. Ladd's tone was just as kind as the first time he'd said the same thing four or five repeats ago. "Otherwise, this will not be comfortable for any of us." It could have sounded like a threat, if he hadn't been saying it so much, his warning had become amused interest.

The problem was there was too little examination room, and far too many of us. Hado had refused to shrink down to kitten size, and was full brute—nearly seven feet of muscle with a deadly scowl.

Abbi remained child size, still wrapped in the heavy wool healing blanket. She stood next to Hado, holding his hand like she'd just found him in a crowded train station and wasn't ever going to let go.

Lu stood near the door, glaring like she expected to have to tear apart this tiny examination room with her bare hands to escape. I was eyeing the low table with a healthy dose of distrust.

"It will hold someone your size," Dr. Ladd said. "And it's easier for me if you're on my level, so if everyone would sit down, it will improve my ability to take care of all of you."

"Only Brogan," Lu said from the door.

"If I get checked over, you get checked over." I had lost the argument on which of us would get into one of those paper napkin robes, and currently stood there feeling like a giant sore thumb sticking out in the small room.

Well, fuck it. Time to swallow my own advice. I bent, more stiffly and awkwardly than I'd hoped because of the damn ankle and every other bruise and strain, and dropped into place.

Dr. Ladd was gray-haired, and had what anyone might describe as an actual twinkle in his eyes. He was heavier in the shoulders, shorter in the arms, and about three and a half feet tall.

There had been a lot of names for people of his height over the years, but I was pretty sure the best to describe him was "doctor".

"Progress," he said happily. "Lawrence filled me in on the nature of your injuries. You were in a car accident in the flash flood. A rollover." He was doing the things all doctors did: checking my blood pressure, clipping my finger with an oxygen measuring device, listening to my lungs and telling me to take deep breaths.

"Smoke inhalation," he said, "isn't anything to mess around with. I'm glad you came in." He draped his stethoscope around his neck. "I don't think you've done permanent damage, but your lungs are irritated. Let's look at your eyes next."

He shone a light in my eyes, held up one finger, and told me to look here and there. I had no idea if I passed the test because his fingers were blurry and I couldn't tell how many he was waving in front of my face, but before I could tell him he was making me sick to my stomach, he had already moved around to the back of my head and was pressing on my skull.

I winced, but tried not to make any noise.

"Almost done here. Let me check your foot."

When changing into the paper robe, I'd asked for a damp towel. I'd done what I could to clean the road grime off of my foot, but after all the cussing I'd gone through to get my boot off without passing out from the pain, the foot cleaning had been quick rather than thorough.

Dr. Ladd didn't seem to care about the cleanliness, but focused on manipulating my foot, asking where it hurt, and probing around the bruises.

"Sprained, not broken, so you won't need a cast."

"Good," I said, relieved.

"It's going to take some time to heal, though. It will heal faster if you stay off of it."

I made what I thought was an agreeable sound, but it didn't fool him for a moment.

"You'll wear a brace, and only take it off at night when you sleep. Let's look at those ribs. Just draw the dressing gown down to your waist."

I did so and grunted at the ache that rolled down my back.

He nodded, taking in the massive bruises I was surprised to see.

"Most people don't feel the minor injuries until hours after the accident. Adrenaline, shock, masks the smaller stuff. Does this hurt?" He pressed on my left side.

I shook my head.

"Any sharp pain when you breathe?"

"No."

"That's what I like to hear. Okay, I'm going to give you some medical support for your ankle. But since Lawrence brought you in, I'm assuming you'd also be open to magical treatment?"

"What kind of magical treatment?" Lu asked before I could.

"I have a healer who stops by every once in a while." He walked over to a large, low cabinet. "We like to keep each other up to date on some basic treatment practices. Anti-inflammatories, non-narcotic pain relievers, sleep aids, that sort of thing. She left me a few of her wares." He opened the door, revealing shelves and drawers, some of them labeled, but most of them not.

He tugged a drawer and riffled through the contents before pulling out a small hoop earring made of twine.

"You don't have pierced ears," he said, turning to me. "Would you consider it?"

I shot a look Lu's way. She tipped her head; her face softened with quiet consideration.

"Why should I?"

"It would be the easiest way to use this for your concussion." He pressed the loop of twine against my earlobe.

My unending headache stopped so quickly, I sucked in a fast breath that started a coughing fit. "Gods," I said through the hacking. Then when I could talk again: "That's good."

"You'd look nice with an earring," Lu admitted.

"Or I could just carry it in my pocket."

"It's not strong enough at that distance." He moved it away from my ear and placed it on my shoulder.

The headache steamrollered over my brain. I shaded my eyes against the brightness of the lights.

"Will it just block the pain, or will it also help heal his concussion?" Lu moved away from the door and stood next to me, her hand between my shoulder blades.

"She said it aides in healing, but it's not an overnight fix. More of a time-release remedy. Slow, but effective."

"And it's for concussions?"

"Yes. She's working on one for migraines, which she assures me is a more difficult thing to treat."

"Once he's healed, what do we do with the earring?"

"I didn't say I wanted to get my ear pierced."

"You can keep it. I don't know if it will retain its healing magic or if it will be drained. If you don't want to keep it, please return it to me. I will give it back to her, and perhaps she will be able to recharge it."

"Not sure I want a hole in my ear," I mumbled.

"We'll do it." Lu gently squeezed my shoulder.

It wasn't like her to trust strangers, but she had a sharp instinct for someone who was trustworthy. Apparently, she trusted this man.

"Do you pierce ears, doc?" I asked.

"Not professionally, but I can get it done."

"Which ear?" I asked Lu. "You're gonna see it more than I will."

Her gaze shifted across my face, deciding. "Left. Unless it matters?" she asked Dr. Ladd.

"Either works. Just need an earlobe."

"Left it is," I agreed.

The doctor might not pierce ears for a living, but he could take it up as a side job and make a mint.

He gave me a brace for my ankle, offered a crutch, which I refused, and then sent me back to the narrow dressing room to change into my clothes that stank of smoke.

When I came out, Hado and Abbi were gone, leaving just me and Lu and the doctor.

"Ready?" Lu asked.

"No, I'm not ready. Have you let the doctor look at you?"

Lu started toward the door. "I'm not the one who was hurt."

"Lula."

There were a lot of ways I could say her name. A lot of ways I had said it over the years. Most of them were in longing. Sometimes frustration. Only so very occasionally in reproach.

She stopped, turned, and crossed her arms over her chest. The raised eyebrow added to her message of general displeasure.

"You're injured," I went on. "You hit your head in the rollover. You were bleeding. There's another pain we should ask for his help with."

"A doctor," she stated.

"Yes, a doctor."

"You know how many doctors I've let treat me in all these years?"

"Yes." It was damn few. Most didn't even know what she was, much less how to care for her.

"No. I'll heal. Faster than you."

I knew how this argument would end—she'd walk out of here and endure the pain from her head injury and her hunger for blood. This was her choice. I couldn't force her to let the doctor look at her, but that didn't mean I couldn't ask for some support.

"Do you carry any blood here, Doc?" I asked.

"That's an unusual request," he said, like it really wasn't all that unusual. "What type of blood?"

"I'm not sure it matters. Maybe doesn't even have to be human. Maybe you have animal blood? Or could point us toward a butcher shop where we could get something fresh?"

Lu hadn't moved, but everything about her was different. She was the love of my life, a clever, determined, strong woman. But she was something else too, something that wasn't human.

I was reminded of that in moments like this.

She looked like a predator, a bird of prey that could see the beating heart of a rabbit ten miles off and had already sharpened her claws for the kill.

"I have blood in the cooler," Dr. Ladd said, like this was the most normal conversation to have with a patient. Maybe it was for the kinds of patients he welcomed through his doors. Even monsters needed a few stitches or a bullet removed now and then.

"I don't keep much on hand," he went on, walking toward Lu, toward the door, as if she wasn't anything to be afraid of. "O negative. One bag is all I can spare. Will that hold you?"

Lu didn't even seem to be aware he was talking, her gaze on me alone.

"Yes," I said. "That will help, thank you. We have cash."

"We'll settle the bill. I'm not concerned. Wait here a moment."

Lu shifted to the side slightly so he could leave the room. She held my gaze.

"We're a team," I reminded her. "You wouldn't have let me leave without the ankle brace or the earring, which, I have to say, I still can't believe you talked me into getting my ear pierced."

Her breathing was shallow and fast, eyes unblinking, every one of her senses tracking the kill.

I wasn't sure she could hear me.

"You were in a car accident. You were hurt. And you haven't had blood in months. Your body is working hard to heal. Let's make sure you can heal, Lula."

I stood in front of her and could smell the smoke on her clothes and skin. But beneath that, I could smell the fragrance that was all her: rose and honey.

I'd seen her like this before, especially in the early days after the attack, when she was struggling to control her changed body and her new life bound to the Route.

Over the years, she'd become an expert in managing her need for blood. She didn't crave it now, and only needed it when her body had been under heavy stress and was stretched too thin to heal.

In those times, she became more the monster she had been changed into than the woman she'd been born as. She became something that didn't think like a human, didn't react or act like a human.

She became hunger.

Times like that didn't happen often, but they did happen.

Like now. Like right now.

I reached for her, because how could I not, and took her hand in mine. "Lula, my love. Are you with me? I need you to see me. To really see me. Here. Real. Your husband. Brogan Gauge."

Something shifted in her, deep and seismic. I held my breath to see which way the scales would tip.

She trembled as if a great sea change rolled through her. Clarity returned to her eyes, and the harshness of the monster within dissolved away by bits, her humanity seeping back into the amber glow of them.

"I know your name." Her voice was a rasp.

"Yeah?" I squeezed her hands gently, stepping even

closer. "Because you love me? Because you've been in love with me forever? All your days?"

"Yes," she whispered, her shoulders slowly softening, the confusion easing. "I love you."

"I love you, Lula Gauge," I said, just as I always would.

"Don't let go." It was quiet, her request. A faint plea, as if she'd been swimming hard against the tide and had only just spotted land.

So I held on, just as I always would. Because I'd had loved her forever. All my days.

CHAPTER SEVEN

"It's a giant bottle." Abbi's voice was still a little wobbly, as if she had to work to fill each word with air. "And it's glowing."

The sixty-six feet tall statue of a soda bottle that stood outside Pops 66 Soda Ranch—a gas station, restaurant, and gift shop that offered every soda brand and style under the sun—was hard to miss. It was night now, the day having lasted a year, and all I wanted was a flat surface where I could snore my way into oblivion.

But the seer was waiting for me here—if I believed my dreams, and if I believed Lawrence—and Headwaters wanted Lula to call.

We'd had the truck towed, and paid for a local shop to do the repairs it needed, both inside and out. They had to order some parts, and were already backlogged, so waiting around for the truck to be fixed wasn't in the cards.

We borrowed a car—an early model SUV that looked like a small station wagon—from one of

Lawrence's friends, gave the woman money for her generosity, though she'd tried to refuse it several times. The worn seats were stained, and the hard surfaces had cracked from UV exposure.

It had a hell of a lot more sitting room than the truck. I tried to convince myself it was more practical than Silver, but the pervasive stink of damp and mold was making me miss the truck, cramped seating room or not.

Lu won the who-will-drive argument, so I was in the passenger seat. Now and then she'd glance over at me watching her, roll her eyes and say: "Still fine." She'd repeated that for miles.

Lorde had sprawled out across the rear bench seat and had slept the whole way.

Hado and Abbi sat in the center seats, Hado still in his human form, Abbi still wrapped in the healing shroud. Her color was better, and her eyes bright, but she was still moving slowly, as if trying to steer around a pain she wasn't used to.

Lu had drunk the bag of blood the doctor had given her with a blank expression that anyone who didn't know her might think meant she didn't have any strong feelings about the action.

But I knew her. I knew how much she hated giving in to a part of her she despised, a weakness that was no fault of her own.

Dr. Ladd sent us on our way, satisfied we were better than when we'd arrived.

Which had left the question of what to do with the

storage unit: should we take all the items out of it, or leave the illusion and hope it held up?

We'd gambled on the illusion. Lawrence said he'd check back on it for us over the next few weeks.

"Not sure why you're doing us the favor," I'd told the druid as everyone piled into the borrowed car.

Lawrence shrugged, but his smile was a thousand watts. "Miss Woodbury is a friend. She wanted me to take care of you while you were passing through, and the storage unit is a part of that. I'll get a crew of people —friends—out there to rebuild the door so the owners don't get too curious. We can do it on the down low. You'll want to stop by again soon to sort out the things that need to be kept, and deal with the things that are ruined and need to be thrown away, buried, or otherwise neutralized."

It was nice to talk to someone who understood what life with magic was like.

We'd left him with enough money to handle the repairs, and extra to replenish the stones and plants he'd used to help us.

And now we were here, in Arcadia, Oklahoma, staring at a giant neon soda pop bottle.

"She said she'd meet us inside," I said.

Lu pulled into a parking spot under a tree, not too close to the building. "Headwaters wants me to call in an hour."

"Seer first?" I asked.

She hesitated, then nodded. "Let's go inside."

"Can I come?" Abbi asked, sounding just as young as she looked.

"I don't see why not. Hado?" I asked.

He wanted to say no, I could see it all over him. Instead, he rolled his shoulders. His shirt became a dark button down with a vaguely Hawaiian design of clouds and moons and ocean waves, and his pants became jeans.

He also had a pair of sunglasses dark enough to hide his unusual eyes.

"Oh," Abbi said. "You're being a tourist, aren't you? I like that. I should be a tourist too." She dug around in her backpack, which was never far from her, and pulled out a pair of oversized hot pink plastic sunglasses, which she settled on her face.

They were comically large. Clown-school large. She grinned at me, pleased with herself. "Can I have a soda pop?"

"Yes," Lu said.

"Can I have ten?"

"No," I said.

Abbi giggled and scooted out the door after Hado. "What about Lorde?" she asked.

"Lorde doesn't like soda pop," I said.

Lorde lifted her head at the sound of her name and yawned, her fuzzy tail thumping.

"We'll bring you back a treat, girl," I said. The brace on my foot made walking a little slower than I wanted, but I was getting the hang of it.

Lu made sure all the windows were rolled down a good several inches, allowing the cooling air to circulate for Lorde, who of course also had water. If Lorde was in any distress, Lu would hear her bark or whine.

Which reminded me. "Do you hear it now?" I asked Abbi, who held Hado's hand. They looked enough alike most people would expect them to be father and daughter.

"The soda pop?" she asked. "Why? Does it sing?"

"No—why would you think soda sings?"

"You said there was every kind of soda here. Maybe there's singing kind and dancing kind. Maybe some explode."

It was strange to think that even though Abbi was centuries older than me, she didn't have a good grasp on something as commonplace as a bottle of sugary beverage.

"Different kinds means flavors," I said, "not the ways they perform."

"Oh," she said, taking that information in. "No singing?"

"No singing."

"I knew that."

I was pretty sure she didn't, and tried to catch Hado's eyes to see how he reacted to her statement, but those sunglasses hid his limited expressions.

"I was asking," I said, trying to bring this back to what I needed to know, bring it back to the important thing, "if you can hear the book."

"The spell book?"

"Yes."

She stopped walking and tipped her face up, sniffing the air. "Maybe?"

It wouldn't have been a problem if we weren't

standing in front of the door with three people trying to exit and two behind us wanting to enter.

I tugged on her free hand, propelling her into the shop.

Inside was a lot cooler than outside. It was also lit nice and bright, Danny and the Juniors on the speakers telling us all to go to the hop.

The two-story wall of windows slanted inward, leaning like a carefully balanced card house. The windows rose floor to ceiling, each lined with metal and glass shelves, upon which were row after row of soda bottles, grouped by color. It was an altar, a stage, a deconstructed, stained-glass tower of sugar and carbonation presented as an unwavering pledge to the soda obsessed.

Straight ahead and taking up the middle space of the shop was a diner-type counter with little round stools the color of cotton candy. An aisle ran down between the counter and tables with booth seating. Behind the counter was a stainless steel working grill where a couple of cooks were going all out, giving tourists and locals a show.

Soda fountains, machines, and memorabilia filled the counter space.

Beyond that, short metal shelves stuffed with candy also offered T-shirts, toys, shot glasses, and anything that could carry the Pops logo, a soda logo, or a Route 66 logo.

Empty cardboard soda pop carriers were faced at the end of aisles, ready for shoppers to mix and match.

Against the back wall of the shop hummed a

blockade of glass-door coolers filled with—of course —soda.

I spotted a few open tables to the right, tucked up beneath the leaning windows, and steered us that way.

The slick glass coolness of the space, the clean manufactured feeling of it all, was overridden by the smell of grilled cheese, fried potatoes, burgers, and a soup that made my mouth water.

Abbi was sniffing loud enough, I glanced down at her.

"I'm hungry for that smell," she said, trying to get back to the grill as Hado guided her forward. "And soda pop. That smell and soda pop. Can I have it?"

"Let's find a table," I said, "then we'll order."

We settled beneath the slanted windows, Abbi perched right under the glass shelves, craning her neck so she could look up and up through the colorful bottles stacked to the highest rafters.

Hado sat next to her, angling his big shoulders, so she was mostly hidden from the rest of the place.

I wanted to do the same thing with Lula. Wanted her near the window so I could be between her and everyone in the shop. But instead of insisting, I waited for her to pick a chair.

She moved past me with a soft chuckle, knowing very well what was going through my mind, and settled across from Abbi near the window, leaving me the outer chair.

"I want that one at the very top." Abbi removed her sunglasses and pointed upward.

Hado considered it and stood.

"No," I said. "Those are decoration. We can order fresh cold soda."

A moment later, the server showed up. She was dressed in a white button-down shirt and pants, black shoes, black belt, and black bow tie. It was a modern take on the original soda jerk uniform.

"Hi, folks, are you ready to order? Our root beer bread pudding is really swell."

Really swell hadn't been in style for decades.

The girl couldn't be a day over seventeen, with her big smile and bouncy brown hair tucked behind her ears. But there was a sparkle in her eyes that said she was in on the joke and liked it.

Probably just working a Joe job until she could head off to college.

"Swell, huh?" I asked, spinning the laminated card that served as a menu my way.

"The bee's knees."

"Bee's knees," I grumbled.

Lu dropped her hand under the table and rested it on my thigh.

We'd been alive when that slang was real, when it was modern, when it was fresh. Hearing it used as an old-timey joke was a little rough on my sense of place in the world.

It was one more reminder that time ticked and ticked, each second a whittling knife shaving off a little more life, carving breath and body down to sticks, twigs, ash.

Lu squeezed my thigh, maybe sensing my mood.

"Medium rare burger and fries," Lu ordered for me,

"grilled cheese sandwich," she ordered for Abbi, "and an extra order of fries. We'll also take two root beer bread puddings. What flavor of soda do you want?" she asked Abbi.

"All of them?"

The server chuckled. "Do you have a favorite flavor? A favorite candy or fruit?"

"I like grass. And clover." Her eyes widened, as if she'd just remembered people who looked like little girls didn't eat grass.

"We have grass soda," she said, making a note on the pad. "I don't think I have clover, though. Something else you want to try? Honey? Butter?"

Abbi's eyes were still wide. "Strawberry?" she asked hopefully, like it was some kind of rare treat.

"Grass and strawberry got it. Anyone else?"

"Moxie," Lu said.

"Got any Brownie Root Beer?" I asked.

"You bet your bippie, we do."

"Better follow that up with a coffee, black," I added.

"Anything for you?"

Hado, still wearing his sunglasses, shook his head.

The server left, and the music switched to the Chordettes singing about lollipops. Someone in the place was whistling along with it. Cheerfully, beautifully. Not too loud, but getting louder.

Coming down the aisle toward us was the owl woman, Miss Woodbury, the seer. Just like in the visions, she wore wide-legged pants under a skirt, layers of shirts, some flannel, some button down, all faded and soft: dusty denim, sage, cinnamon.

She whistled and danced, a sort of herky-jerky slide and skip, that made her cloud of white hair sway and wave, and set the beads, stone, and wood hoops around her wrists and up her skinny forearms chiming, like the soft maraca of a spring rain.

A few people glanced her way—she wasn't invisible—but no one seemed bothered by a woman well into her three-digit years, bopping down the aisle, whistling a tune.

She stopped at our table and rapped her gnarled knuckles on the top of it three times.

The song ended and the drone of a football game on the flat screen on the back wall simmered over the hum of the coolers.

"Brogan Gauge," she said, her voice creakier than I'd remembered. "There you are. I've been waiting for you."

"Miss Woodbury," I said.

"Oh now, we're friends. Or we might be, depending on how this goes." She squinted, thinking. "Call me Eunice. We can start there."

"I'm here like you asked." I stood, and yes, I was using my size to make a point: I wasn't going to let her hurt me, or my family. "Whatever you have to say, you can say it now."

"Well, I'd like to sit down, if that's all right with you. Old woman like me. Don't move like I used to."

"You were dancing."

"That was ages ago."

"Minutes ago," I said.

She nodded. "That too. That too." Then she sort of

squeezed around me and folded layer by layer like a telescope onto my chair, sighing like she hadn't been off her feet in years. "Would you look at all that soda pop? Just look at this place."

The music came on again, the Beach Boys getting around, and Miss Woodbury—Eunice—tapped her finger in time.

"Have I told you why I called you here yet?" she asked.

I traded a glance with Lu over her head. Lu just raised one eyebrow.

"You mentioned a few things in the vision."

"One vision?" she asked.

"There were two. You only seemed to want to talk in the second one."

"Ah-yah, I'm that way sometimes, sometimes. So what I said in those visions is true, as much as any other time, but what you ask *now*, what I answer *here*, is real. This is where you start forward again, Brogan Gauge, on this old road you've been following."

She was still tapping, her bracelets keeping the beat. Her eyes had gone clear and sharp, a light in them growing.

"Why is the god bad?" Abbi blurted.

Eunice blinked, and blinked some more, her fingers losing the beat of the song. It took her a second to recover, to get that finger tapping again to the Beach boys still gettin' around. When she did, she seemed to see Abbi for the first time, and focused on her.

I didn't know if I liked that.

Hado clearly didn't. He placed his big hand on Abbi's shoulder.

It was a subtle thing, but when he touched her, it snapped the two of them into something more than what they were separately. They were the same, each their own person, but together they were heightened, defined, the magic, or power, or supernaturalness of what they were enhanced.

"Moon Rabbit." Eunice nodded. "Shadow. Is that the question you ask this time? Exactly?"

Abbi tipped her head. "Yes. Why is the god bad?"

Eunice jangled the beads on her wrist. "These things, gods, are always wanting. This one seeks reparations. This god was slighted, power refused when the book was bound. Late to the party, I suppose.

"A god can create anything, control anything within their power. But this is not within the god's power. Therefore, it is valuable. In claiming it, using it or destroying it, the god would have power and possession of something no other god possessed.

"That thing, that book, created by so many gods, is valuable simply for its impossibility of ever existing once, or ever existing again. If the god is clever enough, the lock and key will be easy to find, easy to break, then the god will have access to all the gods' powers. Reality will change."

Goosebumps rolled down my neck, and my stomach clenched. Cupid was a god of connections and destruction. He wanted us to find that book, and until this moment, I would have been happy to drop it in his hands and never see him or the book again.

Now I was wondering what giving a god that book would do. What kind of damage could be done to the world, to the people I loved.

"How do you know that?" Abbi asked.

Eunice spread her hands, beads sighing. "Because I am what I am."

Whatever that meant.

"Why did I fall?" Abbi pressed. "You said I fell."

Eunice lowered her hand, fingers hovering above the table.

I held my breath. There needed to be a song. Somehow I knew there needed to be a song for Eunice to tap to, a way she could remain anchored in this reality, this possibility. Or maybe a way she could remain clear-sighted beneath the scattershot futures shifting under the waves of free will.

She was song, or connected to song in a deep way I could sense, but didn't have words for. What did she mean when she said she was what she was? A seer?

The sound of a *click*, like a record arm swinging to drop a needle into a vinyl groove, filled the store.

But there was no one playing records here.

Eunice's finger dropped, sharp nail tapping the Formica, and a new song poured out over the speakers, this one a little slower, but strong: The Five Satins were crooning what they were going to do in the still of the night.

"You must answer that, Moon Rabbit," Eunice said. "I see…I can feel so many reasons you fell, so many times. Loneliness? Curiosity? You were looking for something too. Have you found it?"

"They have grass soda," Abbi said, as if that were any kind of an answer.

"Yes," Eunice agreed. "They do."

"And, I don't know." Abbi picked up the huge sunglasses in the middle of the table, her gaze darting to Lu, then to me. "They have other things too. Nice things. Nice…people."

"Yes," Eunice agreed. "They do. Do you understand?"

"I don't know. I just…you said I fell for him." She frowned, then leaned her head toward Hado, who looped his arm over her shoulder, taking her scant weight.

Eunice still stared at some far-off horizon, her finger rising and dropping on beat. "Maybe I was right."

"Who do you work for?" Lu asked.

I startled, because I hadn't thought of that, but I nodded. It was a good question. A great question.

"No one. Well, not as how you are asking. No one told me to find you other than my own self. No one pays me for my time, since time and me are a mess, mostly."

"No god?" Lu asked.

Eunice shifted her way, the light through the window throwing broken-glass colors like flower petals across her snow white hair. "No god, lost daughter. No monster, no human. I follow my own road, pay my own tolls. The book is not mine, nor do I want it."

"What do you want?" I asked.

It was her turn to startle. Her finger lost the beat again, and it took several more for her to pick it up. But now, oh, now she was smiling as she twisted toward me.

"That, Brogan Gauge, is exactly what I wanted to hear."

She snapped her fingers.

Everything in the shop stopped.

Lu, Abbi, Hado, our server who was coming our way with a tray of food, the kids running down the candy aisle, the two middle-aged men loading up on soda flavors that could only be intended as a dare—all froze.

Eunice stood. "There isn't much time in this time, not even a whole beat. I need to show you something. Quickly."

"You need to snap me back into the world."

"I will, this is…" She pressed her fingers over her lips, then tried again. "Brogan, if I'm right, and this has been passed down to me by those of sight and song before me…mothers, grandmothers, aunties…Our big puzzle unsolved. Years. Decades. We've been watching. Looking."

"For the book?"

"For that, yes." She took a step away, stopped, her hands on her hips. "You have to walk with me. I can't drag you to the truth, this old body."

"I'm not leaving them behind."

"Of course you're not. This is still here, this is still now, it's just a bit more. A step will do. It shows intent, it shows agreement, and that's the thing I need from you."

"I've never heard of a seer who can stop time, or fall a person into the cracks between time, who needs permission to say a thing."

"Yes, well, we all aren't what we look like. You look

like a stubborn ass who might not do what I've asked, but maybe there's a sensible man down in your bones."

She waited. I waited. Then she sighed. "It's important. It will help you keep Lula safe."

She was manipulating me, but my gut said she was also telling the truth.

I didn't want to go with her, but I wanted to know whatever was so important, she'd stop time.

I spread my hand and pressed fingertips against the top of the table to keep myself aligned with this reality, to stay grounded. It was an old trick from my spirit days.

Then I took one step forward with my good foot.

The world swirled, edges going soft, colors melting into fog. We stood in something that felt like a temple, felt like green, like spring, even though there was nothing I could see past the vague rolling of gold-drenched fog and darkness.

Eunice stood in front of me, a fountain, no, a bowl of water set on spindly legs, tall enough it came to her waist between us.

Eunice wasn't Eunice anymore. Or rather, she wasn't *just* Eunice.

Younger, certainly, and to my surprise, shorter.

Her eyes, though, were deep, echoing other women's eyes, her features blurred with the overlay, the underlay of others: finer, thicker, older, younger. She was a hundred women, a thousand, each paper-thin and stacked upon the other to create this most outwardly Eunice.

Eunice who raised her hands over her head, a never ending slide of bracelets chiming down her arms.

Eunice who said, "This is it."

Eunice who winked and snapped her fingers, hands still raised above her head.

The gold fog rolled as if a gentle breeze had slipped into the space with us, like the draft of a door opening.

Behind Eunice stood a woman, taller, thicker, with dark, heavy hair. And then behind her was another woman, back and back, disappearing forever into the fog, tall and short, notes written across an endless measure, until it was only Eunice standing in that skin. Just one note, but integral to the song.

"I am, we are, many names and one," she said. "Seer, muse. We are Euterpe, of music, of lyric poetry, the giver of delight." She lowered her hands. "A lot of other names, a lot of other times, but we are we, and I have been called by you to help. So I'm here. Helping."

"I didn't call you."

The paper thin visions of women held very still.

The golden clouds froze.

Then Eunice scratched at the back of her neck. "No, I'm pretty sure you called me. Had to be you, Brogan Gauge. You've been god-touched and thrust back into the living. You're just the sort of soul who would be brooding and lamenting, and needing some help."

"I didn't call you. Didn't dream you, didn't invite you into a vision. I don't know why you're so set on me, Eunice, but it isn't because I need you."

She waved off the women behind her. "This isn't going to work. I'll talk to him. Give me a minute."

The other women, the sheet music score of what

Eunice was, or could be, faded away, like a chorus going silent.

"You wouldn't guess it," Eunice said, looking much more relaxed. "But I never have any trouble talking people into listening to me. The whole multiple-me thing is very impressive."

I crossed my arms over my chest and waited.

That made her cackle. "Okay, so you might guess it. You are a man with clear eyes, Brogan. Few who walk the world can say the same, though, yes, there are some. So. Here is the truth: I need you to find something for me. In return, I'm going to guide you, warn you, meddle in your knowledge of your future so that you generally end up better for it."

"I don't find things for people."

She chuckled. "You most certainly do. You always have. Lula does too. It's why you're here, well, certainly part of the reason. She is going to call that collector. Headwaters? Or maybe she already has. She's going to offer that collector an item, something that fits in her pocket, and Headwaters is going to tell her something… something she won't like. Or something that will worry her."

"Anyone could guess those things," I said. "Just like anyone could find whatever you're looking for. Ask someone else. We don't have time to take on more."

She nodded, and the beads dangling at her ears rattled like dry beans in a cup.

"You do not. For perhaps the first time in your life, you don't have time, Brogan Gauge."

I shouldn't respond, I shouldn't bite, because I knew

what this was. This was her drawing me in, wanting me to ask about a future she might or might not be seeing.

"You can't even tell me what's in Lu's pocket."

"Harmonica."

I stared at her for a minute. She stared right back.

"You can't even tell me what Headwaters' is going to say."

"We can find another source. Your services, while being exemplary, are no longer needed. This last transaction will be the final transaction."

Chills rolled up and down my arms. She had recited that easily, in a flat tone devoid of her usual voice. It could be a trick.

She could be a trick.

But my gut said she was not lying.

"What do you want found?"

"You agree to find it for me?"

"No. I want to know what you've lost."

She winced. "It's not lost. It's been stolen."

I waited.

"A long time ago. It's not a needle in a haystack, but close. Very close to that." She looked away, over my shoulder, then back to me, stalling.

"I'd rather you agree first," she said. "It's…easiest, no…cleanest? Yes, it's the most successful future if you agree. Because past this moment things will happen, choices will be made, and then, well, it all changes then."

"I can't agree to find something for you. We're committed to other things."

"Yes, yes. The spell book of the gods. I know." She

pinched the bridge of her nose. "No one tells you vision is exhausting, did you know that? No one explains how difficult it is to sort through all the grains of sand pouring through the hourglass of time, how hard it is to spot the correct grain that is the inevitable future. It's like trying to catch a handful of wind, or plucking the right drop of water out of the ocean.

"Hard," she said, letting her hands drop. "I'm telling you." She dug fingers into her lower back, leaned backward in a stiff stretch. A couple bones popped. "This future stuff is not for the weak willed. So, let's compromise. That way neither of us gets exactly what we want, but both of us are better off in some manner.

"I need something the god has stolen. It's an ancient item, and it belongs to me and mine. In the god's hands…" She shook her head. "Not good. The god will destroy the world and then use it against decent people. Against a decent world. I am putting my wager that you're a good man and won't want that to happen.

"So. I'm going to tell you something very true and very real. If you still want nothing to do with me, that's fine, that's fine. But if you want me to help you, or even if you just want to help the world, then you'll need to help me.

"You know what I want. I want you to find something for me. Here is my good faith offer. A truth for you. One very clear truth of your future.

"The god wants you dead. The moment you find the spell book and put your hand on it, the god will kill you and then Death himself will come for your soul."

CHAPTER EIGHT

I t should have shocked me, hearing I might die, but I'd spent a lot of time being halfway to the grave anyway, and Death himself, as Eunice had said, had never once come calling.

"I'm assuming there are loopholes in that prediction," I said.

She blinked. "What are you talking about? I just told you a true thing that will happen in your future if you don't change your path, change your decisions. Didn't you hear me? Didn't you hear the words I said?"

"I heard the words. But I've heard predictions before. We put years into tracking down any priestess, soothsayer, or fortune-teller who could tell us what we could do to change our fate. Nothing they told us came true how any of the tellers said it would. So yes, I heard your words. I don't think they are as reliable as they seem on the surface."

Her eyebrows shot up. "You are calling me a liar?"

"Not lies. You said it was the truth, and I believe it is

the truth as *you* see it at this moment. But there hasn't been any hand dealt to Lula or me we haven't had some way of turning to our advantage. Words of a prophet aren't always what they seem. They might be a hell of a lot more. Or less."

"I told you a god is using you. Doesn't that bother you?"

"We made a deal with the god, and we're going to see through our side of it."

She frowned. "You're making a mistake, Brogan. I can't…I don't know how I can say it any plainer than I have. You have a chance to make a different choice. A choice that will help me. If you forget about the spell book and walk away from the god, things will be…well, I can't say they will be easy, but I don't see your death down that road. Not soon. Not *as* soon."

"I won't be talked into going against my word by you. I'm not afraid of death, would have welcomed it some years."

She gave a little cackle that was surprisingly musical. "Oh, I can see there will be no talking you into anything." She looked me up and down. When her gaze met mine again, the awareness of a thousand seers shone in her eyes.

"You will change this world, Brogan Gauge. You and Lula both. The family you choose, the family you make. With our help, without it. But heed our warning. The god will betray you, and that sorrow will break Lula's heart beyond mending."

She clapped her hands once.

It was a soft sound, like a wooden box closing, a

door slipping the latch, a heavy stone thudding into deep sand.

Then music wound back up to speed, like a turntable switching gears, the fog clearing as if it had never been there.

The smell of hot grease, charred meat, and root beer filled my nostrils.

The Formica tabletop was cool under my fingertips.

Eunice was gone, not even a bead left behind.

"Brogan?" Lula gave me a funny look, already halfway out of her chair, concern creasing her forehead.

"Oh no," Abbi said, twisting so she could see the door. "They're here."

Like a square peg in a round hole, I was having a hard time clicking into place with this reality. For a long moment, too long, I fought off a sweaty panic attack. Thoughts of being out of step in time, out of step in the flow of the real world, of not *existing* like a real living human, burned like wildfire through my brain.

It was nightmare fuel for me, too long a spirit, too long existing as *nothing*— drifting and ineffectual—while Lu was right there, in my reach and forever beyond it.

I couldn't do that again. I refused to do that again.

I took a deep breath, tried to calm my mind, my nerves screaming that everything was wrong, everything was *very* wrong, that I had no control, had no power to make it even slightly right again.

I slapped my palm flat on the cold, slightly greasy table.

The shock of it, the pricking pain, cleared my

thoughts. Square peg hammered into the round hole of this moment.

I was here. I was real. I was alive.

"So many," Abbi said.

A couple dozen middle-aged people, some white, some darker skinned, strode into the place. Bikers, from the jeans, leather chaps, and matching riding jackets.

A gang?

A club, I corrected myself. Most bikers were in a club, and this one must have been riding Route 66 judging from the animated conversations and laughter. The group split, some sifting down the aisles to the soda selections, others threading over to the mementos and Route 66 souvenirs, and the rest wandering up to the counter to order food.

"Oh," Abbi said.

Oh, indeed. At the end of the crowd was a man.

Well, not a man. A god. Cupid, who liked to go by the name Bo, fit right in with the bikers. Just like the others, he wore boots, black denim, black leather chaps, and a black leather jacket. Unlike the others, a pastel pink heart pierced by a silver arrow was stitched into his jacket, right over where his heart might be, and on each shoulder, white wings.

He was bald, bearded, ears studded with glinting jewels, arms and hands tattooed, and he was coming our way.

Lu's hand wrapped around my wrist, tense. She was worried and must know that something had happened to me.

"Fine," I said, my voice a little rough. I cleared my throat. "I'm fine. I'll tell you later."

We were both standing, but Abbi and Hado remained sitting. Hado hadn't even turned to look at the god, and I wondered if he could see through Abbi's eyes, since he was her shadow.

"Lula and Brogan," Cupid said. "Good to see you here. May I join you?"

My breathing was still a little too fast. Some of that was the last tatters of the near panic attack. Some of that was Eunice's words.

The god, this god was going to betray us.

The god, this god was going to kill me.

And it would break Lula's heart beyond mending.

Cupid stilled, his sharp eyes holding my gaze. "I don't know the future," he said, easy, like calming an animal. "But I won't betray you."

"What?" Lula said. "What are you talking about?"

"Eunice," I said.

He nodded. "She knows the future. But there are many futures. In none of them do I go back on my word. In none of them."

A tremor worked its way through my body. A god's word, his intent, was a powerful thing.

But Eunice had not been lying to me. I knew that too.

Somewhere between these two powerful beings was the truth—well, many truths—but one of them would be ours.

"Let's sit," Cupid said, and the table was now a little

larger, just enough for another chair to be available at the end.

"Why are you here?" Lu asked.

"I'll tell you," he said mildly, "but we might as well have a soda while we talk." He took the new chair, and a server showed up with a tray with five sodas.

"Thank you," Cupid said.

The server placed the drinks on the table and left.

I tugged on Lu's hand, drawing her down into her seat as I took the other open chair where Eunice had been moments before.

"You're Cupid." Abbi peeked out from behind Hado, keeping the bulk of his body between her and the god.

"I am. Please call me Bo. What should I call you, little rabbit?"

"Abbi," she said, quietly. "This is my Hado."

"Abbi," he said, "pleased to meet you. Pleased to meet you, Hado."

Hado gave the god a judgmental slow blink that was very cat-like.

The corner of Bo's mouth quirked up. "I am also pleased Brogan and Lula found you. I heard you. I sent them."

Hado sat a little straighter and tipped his head, looking at the god through fresh eyes.

"Did he really do that?" Abbi asked.

"He told us to find you," I said. "You told us to find Hado."

Cupid nodded. "That is also true."

"Why are you here?" Lula asked. She hadn't touched the drink. None of us had.

"I know the seer has been interested in you." Cupid sat back and tapped a finger on the table. "She met you in visions."

"Connections and destruction," I said, naming two of the things his power covered.

"Yes. Her connection to you doesn't worry me."

"She told me you'd betray us," I said.

"I know."

"She told me the moment we found the spell book of the gods for you, you would kill me."

His eyebrows rose and the sparks of light in his diamond ear studs were infinitely small galaxies, spinning. "I made you a promise. Life, or as close to it as I could give you, as long as you looked for the spell book, and helped bring a few people together for me."

I waited. I knew our deal. I also knew gods were dangerous.

And excellent liars.

"Once we find the book?" Lula asked.

"You will continue on as you are—as alive as you are now. Life itself, granting mortal life, is not what my power covers. But promising you will be connected, living flesh, that I can do and have done and will continue to do."

"But you're bad," Abbi said.

Instead of hiding, she leaned forward enough that she could better see him around Hado. "Gods can be tricksters," she said. "I've seen that. Some aren't even what they look like."

"True. Has a god fooled you before, little moon?"

"Yes." Abbi scrunched up her face. "I don't like it, though."

"Do you think I've fooled you and fooled your friends?"

She studied him, holding herself unnaturally still, her eyes wide and unblinking.

The only part of her that was moving at all was her nostrils, just the slightest twitch. She was, of course, not an actual rabbit. She was a power of her own, even if that power was minor compared to the god she was studying.

"I don't think you have," she said quietly. Then she shook her head. "I think you really are Cupid. You make people fall in love."

He smiled and leaned just a bit to pick up one of the sodas: sarsaparilla. "I *help* people fall in love. I can bind people to each other, but the truth is, even a god can't force love. Love is its own power."

"Can you force my friends to find the book you want?"

He tipped the bottle and swallowed before putting it down and running his thumb through the condensation on the glass. "I could force them to serve me, yes. I could bind them to me, and they would not be able to say no to anything I told them to do."

Abbi frowned. "I don't like that."

"I didn't bind them. Not in that way. We entered an agreement, one which," and this he sent my way, "Brogan and Lula can end at any time they wish. You remember that, don't you?"

I did. Of course I did. I was the one who had set that term. But Abbi was watching me like I was a pot about to boil over. I nodded.

"It's true. We can end our agreement at any time."

"So," Cupid asked, "is this when you tell me you want to end our agreement?"

Unlike the seer, nothing about the place changed. The music was still the music, Bobby Darin looking for his dream lover so he didn't have to be alone. The patrons were still the patrons, bikers laughing and taking food outside to eat in the grassy areas, wait staff and cooks shifting it into high gear to make sure everyone was taken care of.

Time was still time, ticking ever forward.

Lu's hand slipped into mine under the table, and I knew her fear. If we backed out of our agreement now, would that end me being here, solid, real, alive beside her? Would he snap his fingers and take away what I'd only now begun to enjoy? Would he make me a spirit again?

"You have put your trust in me," Cupid said. "I've given my word and held to it. Have I done anything to make you doubt me? Have I fallen short of my promises? How have I lost your trust?"

He hadn't. Cupid had been straight with us from the beginning. He wanted us to search for the spell book. He wanted us to find a few people or help a few people connect, people like Abbi and Hado. People like one very annoying werewolf ghost named Valentine, who we'd left at a Crossroads in Missouri. People like a clever computer repair woman and a sunny-faced mechanic in McLean, Illinois.

For a god he had been…kind. Kind to us. Kind, even to Valentine, and now, Abbi.

That wasn't something we were used to.

Our other dealings with gods had been brief and brutal.

"The deal stands," I said, and Lu's hand squeezed mine once, in approval. "It isn't what you've done. As of this moment, I have no quarrel with you. The seer seems to think otherwise. That you will betray us. Deceive us. Kill us."

Abbi made a small sound, and Hado draped his big arm around her.

Cupid's thumb traced the side of the bottle again. "Euterpe is a muse."

Lu leaned forward. "She met him in visions. Tried to tell him the future."

Cupid considered that for a moment. "She isn't a seer in the traditional sense, I suppose. But she knows the music of the universe, can pluck the strings of the future. She has instruments, reeds and brass and bone and skin that carry her power. In them, in her age, in her many selves, she can see possibilities. Some of those possibilities are the future. Or can be the future. She draws the universe's music through mortals, inspires them to hear it, to feel it.

"And when mortals feel that connection…they change the world. Change the future. So yes, in her way, she knows the future, because she plays it through every living thing, and hears it singing in every moment, every decision, every heartbeat.

"Did she tell you what she wanted?" he asked.

"Our services," I said. "To find something stolen from her."

His frown was quick, then gone. "What thing?"

Here it was. The choice to really trust him. And oddly, a memory flashed before my eyes. Cupid knelt in the middle of a dusty road, a small green river snaking past him. The air was heavy, hot at that time of day. Lu was beside me, and our hands, for the first time in almost a hundred years, were clasped skin-to-skin.

Lorde, our sweet dog who had thrown herself in front of a gunman to save Lu, wagged her tail at Cupid, unafraid. She let him pet her. She let him heal her.

He had done those things before settling the deal with us, fed her treats before we'd come to any agreement to work with him.

Kindness.

Not something I'd expect from a being as old as him. Certainly not something I'd expect him to extend to us or our dog. If I had to trust a god, he might be the one who deserved it.

"She didn't say what it was," I said. "Just that the god—you—had it. With it, you would destroy the world and use it against decent people. Against a decent world."

He hummed, then pushed the soda bottles, one at a time, in front of each of us. "Is that the way she said it? 'The god'?"

"Yes."

"She didn't say my name? Any of them? Mention my power? My traits?"

"No." I knew what he was getting at, and I sure as shit didn't like it.

"There are a lot of gods in this world, Brogan. A lot more in the universe." His tone was fatherly, and there was a hint of relief, a little humor too.

I sighed and pulled the soda toward me. "All right. Which god do you think she was talking about?" I took a swig. Blueberries, and something rich like honey that sang to me of spring and sunlight, bloomed across my tongue. It was delicious, and I was certain it wasn't a soda this shop carried, but rather one Cupid had created just for me.

"Could be any god," he said. "If I knew more of what Euterpe wanted, it would help."

"She didn't tell me more. Other than the god would kill me as soon as we found the spell book."

Lu, who had been sipping soda the color of starlight, jerked as if slapped. She placed the bottle that smelled of quince blossoms on the table in front of her, her gaze on Cupid alone.

"What god wants us dead?" she asked.

Cupid gave a short shake of his head. "I don't know the minds of most gods."

"What god wants the spell book enough to kill us for it?" she pressed.

"Either many, or none. It was made so long ago, I don't know that any god remembers it, or cares that it exists."

"You remember it. You know it exists," Abbi said.

"And at least one other does," he agreed.

"Someone who knows we're looking for it," I added.

"Possibly." He drummed blunt fingers on the table.

"Why us?" Lu asked. That was a question we'd both pondered in the weeks since we'd first met Cupid. "There are other people on the road. Others who use magic. Others who are better at finding things. Locating lost magical items. Why did you choose us?"

Cupid's expression was grave. "Because the book had already found you. Out of all the people on this earth, it fell into your hands. There are few who can touch it without suffering the consequences. The book is built to choose who holds it."

I remembered the story of the man in the suit who had given the book to the ghost, Stella, and that he'd told her the book chose its owner.

I could tell Lu wanted to argue with him. The hunter had stolen it from us, hadn't he? But then, there might be a magical workaround for holding the book. Might be magical items that could negate the book's protection.

"Someone burned our storage unit looking for it," Lula said.

Cupid blinked, surprised. "Who?"

"We don't know," she said. "Maybe the same person who ran us off the road and tried to kill us."

Now his head tipped back, and his nostrils flared. I expected the music to pause, time to skip, as it had with Eunice, but reality remained unchanged.

The god though, he was different. Larger, more powerful, less human. He filled the space and gave it a weight as if everything here was rooted in place, immovable as the mountains.

I inhaled and blinked, and Bo once again appeared to be nothing more than a bald, bearded biker, holding a soda.

"When I have an answer," he said, "the right answer to who is trying to kill you, I will tell you. But until then, I will do what I can." He flattened his palm and slid his hand forward to the center of the table. "If any of you need to call me, use this, and I will hear you."

He lifted his hand. I expected something magical, something magnificent, something rare.

"Dimes?" I asked.

Four dimes shiny enough to be newly minted, sat in the center of the table.

"Easy to carry, not valuable enough to steal, and common. Sometimes the most important things are the most ordinary." He smiled softly, and I had a moment to wonder how many lives he must have seen pass by to sound nostalgic over a dime.

Abbi reached for one, but paused, her hand hovering over the coins. "Is there a trick?"

"In how the dimes work?" he asked.

Her wide eyes darted to me, then to Lu. She withdrew her hand. "I...no. Not how they work. Power. Your power makes them work. But if I have one...." She looked down at her lap. "Should I have one? I'm not like them," she mumbled.

"Like them how?"

One shoulder bobbed. "Family."

"Aren't you though?" he asked.

I opened my mouth to answer that, wanting to say yes, but wanting to keep Abbi safe by saying no. I was relieved from my decision by Lula.

"Is this another contract?" Lu asked. "Are these dimes another binding?"

"No, this is a promise. From me." He nodded to the coins. "I will hear you. I will come to you if you call. If you're run off the road again, or in danger, think of me. Or you can literally drop a dime." He waggled his eyebrows. "I'll come to you."

Lu was the first of us to pick up the coin. She inspected it, then dropped it in her pocket. I, not being an idiot, followed suit, and Abbi picked up the last two and handed one to Hado.

"Good," the god said. "Don't be shy about using them. Anything you need, I'm here."

"Which brings me to my question," I said. "Why are you here now?"

"I wanted to meet Abbi and Hado. To know they are well."

Abbi had her mouth open, poised to drop the coin into it and swallow. She caught my look and instead squirmed to bring her backpack to her lap. She fiddled with a zipper and put the coin into a pocket.

"I'm well," she said. "We found Hado, and saved him, and most of the time he's a fluffy cat, and sometimes I can make him purr and I'm happy." Then, a little quieter, "I like Brogan and Lula. I won't leave them if you try to make me."

"I wouldn't tell you to leave them if you're happy."

"You do that, though. Put people together and take them apart."

"I do."

She busied herself with her backpack. "You know I'm not a little girl."

"I do."

"You know I have powers." Here she looked up at him. It was a much older and more powerful being behind her gaze. Her magic was easy to see, the strength of it, different from a god's power, a reflected light instead of a boiling source. But that reflected light came from everywhere, from everything, endless and flowing.

"I do."

She nodded. "I won't let you hurt them."

"Good," he said. "You belong here. But there is another reason I came to speak with you all. Fate is fickle. She's other things too: determined, thoughtful, devious. She is a constant reminder that very few things happen through chance.

"There is a change in the wind. A restless force kicking stones down this old road. I thought I felt it here, in this place, near you. I thought I would arrive and see it in the shadows. I thought it would take you, change you."

He frowned, and I found that I did not enjoy the feeling of knowing a god was troubled, and that those troubles involved me and mine.

"The seer?" Lu asked. "Eunice?"

"No. I know her. I know her music and the songs she won't sing."

There seemed to be a lot of history in that statement, but I wasn't the man who was going to ask what that history might be.

"There is a gathering coming up. I'd like you to go to it." He pulled a flyer out from the inside pocket of his jacket.

He offered it to me, and I unfolded it.

"Route 66 Junk Hunt." I handed the flyer to Lu. "It's in Bristow at the train depot. Why are we going there?"

"I just know you need to make that connection. Need to be there. I think it has to do with the spell book."

"That's oddly specific for a god," I said.

"Gods can be very direct when we want to be."

"Going in blind is my least favorite way to operate. Can you tell us anything else? Are we supposed to meet someone there? Buy something there? Learn something there?"

"Any of those things could happen. You'll go. You'll listen and look. It will become clear then."

"So much for direct," I said.

He smiled, and it was wicked, but also warm, like a bonfire inviting you to lean in just a little closer and promising it wouldn't burn.

"I didn't say gods were *always* direct." He rapped knuckles on the table. "Keep the coins. Call if you need. Until our paths meet again." He stood. "Safe travels, Gauges and family."

Abbi sucked in a happy little breath.

"Safe travels," Lu said.

Cupid strolled out of the shop, moving through the

clumps of people like water around stones. He opened the door and was gone.

"I don't think he's bad," Abbi said. "He gave us money."

"Giving people money doesn't make someone good," Lu said.

"I know. Still." She went back to eating her grilled cheese sandwich.

Somewhere between the out-of-time conversation with Eunice and Cupid showing up, our food had been delivered. My mouth watered.

"Eat," Lu encouraged. "Tell me what Eunice told you."

I did both those things, although the food took priority for the first few bites. The burger was good, and fries better. Even the soda Cupid had ordered for me worked perfectly, sweet against the salt.

Lu listened quietly, but I knew she was worried and angry that she hadn't known I'd slipped through time and faced the muse on my own.

"I hate she took you from me," Lula said.

"She did no such thing. I will always be with you. Always."

I popped a fry in my mouth and chewed, watching her. She scowled at her fries.

"We're both physical now." I reached for her hand under the table, and she laced her fingers through mine. "It means we will be in different places some-times. I trust you to look after yourself, though it kills me if I'm not there with you. I need you to trust me the same."

She inhaled, held it, her chin tipped up, then she nodded once.

"I love you, Lula Gauge. Death himself couldn't keep me from you."

"I love you too, Brogan Gauge. If Death touches you, I'll kill him." She viciously bit a fry in half, but the anger was already draining away.

"I need to call Headwaters," she said after she'd eaten several more fries.

"It can wait."

"No, I don't think it can." She thumbed through icons on her phone and pulled up one that said HEADWATERS.

It was still noisy in the joint. Tennessee Ernie Ford was singing about what sixteen-tons will get you. Lula pressed her phone to one ear, cupping the other ear.

My hearing wasn't as good as hers, but I could make out the ringing, then the slight click of the call going through.

"This is Gauge," Lula said, using her last name as she had from the beginning of working for the mysterious art and magic collector.

A pleasant man's voice asked her to hold, didn't wait for her reply, and then left the call silenced.

Tennessee had one fist of iron and one made of steel. By the time he was really belting out how much he owed the company store, the call clicked again.

A woman's voice said, "Thank you for holding, Gauge. Headwaters hasn't heard from you in over three months. While you are an excellent contact, we can find another source. Your services, while being exemplary, are no longer needed. The last transaction will be the final transaction."

Chills washed over me and my stomach went sour. Those were the exact words Eunice had told me Headwaters would say.

"Unless," the voice went on, "you are still interested in working with us."

Lu's shoulders were tight, but her voice was emotionless when she answered. "The terms of our agreement are still adequate. There is no time frame on our transactions. I was unaware that had changed."

"It hasn't," the woman said quickly. "Headwaters is pleased with your professionalism and excellent procurement abilities. There is no desire on our part to alter the agreement."

The woman waited for Lu to say something. To agree or offer a nicety. Lu didn't speak.

The woman cleared her throat. "There is an item Headwaters is seeking. Of course, we are making you the offer first, but if you refuse, we will approach other contractors."

Lu still didn't speak. There was power in silence. Power in patience.

"If you aren't interested?" The woman volleyed.

"What item?" Lu asked, still in that flat, emotionless tone.

"A book. A very rare book. It is said to have unique qualities."

Unique qualities was code for magic.

There were a lot of magic books in the world. As a matter of fact, any ordinary book in the right reader's hands was magic. A book was a portal to other lands, other lives. It was a private connection, a shared living with people who could not be found anywhere else.

It was an answer to yearning, sustenance to the heart, a balm to the spirit.

But there were some books that were made to carry the hidden knowledge of magic.

My gut clenched, because I knew which rare book with unique qualities they had to be looking for.

"How would I recognize it?" Lu asked.

"It was written for the gods."

"This isn't our agreement. Headwaters buys what I find. I'm not a dog who plays fetch for anyone."

"You will be rewarded. Three times your going rate, if you can find the book."

Lu waited.

"Five times," the woman corrected.

That was a lot of money. Enough Lu wouldn't have to sell magical items for a year or more. But we both knew what book Headwaters wanted, and we had already promised it to a god.

"Does Headwaters know where the book is?"

"Are you accepting the contract?"

I squeezed her hand. She could accept it, get the information Headwaters might have, and simply not hand over the book. Because if we found it, as soon as we found it, we were delivering it to Cupid.

"If I can procure the book you're looking for, I will contact Headwaters."

That wasn't exactly what the woman wanted to hear.

I could tell by the intake of breath on the other end of the phone. "Perhaps we will find another picker."

"Are you ending the contract, then? Releasing my first-find services to other buyers?"

The silence on the line dragged for several beats, the sounds of the shop filling the time. Laughter, chatter, and Neil Diamond telling us about Cherry and the ways she can move him.

"Bristow," the woman said. "We have a lead that it may be in Bristow."

Lu squeezed my fingers back. We had a lead. Bristow. The same town Cupid had wanted us to go to. The town with the Junk Hunt.

All signs were pointing at Bristow, and every one of those signs flashed red.

CHAPTER NINE

Bristow wasn't far, but it was late and the Junk Hunt didn't start until tomorrow. We cruised the town in our borrowed SUV hoping Abbi would hear the book, but she kept shaking her head, until frustrated, she pulled the healing blanket over her head and burrowed next to Hado, unwilling to say anything more.

She was tired. We were all tired. We hadn't had time to recover from the accident, from the fire, or from the healing.

Add to that, a seer, a god, and whatever kind of power play Headwaters was trying to pull, and the overall feeling that something was wrong, that we were either falling into line with a fate out of our control or just plain falling into a trap, put us all on edge.

"Motel," Lu said. "Soft beds, good sheets."

"Field not too far out of town," I countered. "Trees. Looks like a clear night."

"Trying to stay off grid at this point won't matter," Lu said. "And I'd like a shower."

"You just had a shower, what? Yesterday?"

She frowned, but when she threw me a look and saw my smile, her eyebrows rose. "Daily, Brogan. If circumstances allow, I like a shower daily."

"Near the Junk Hunt?" I asked, stretching my leg and wincing. The earring was doing a hell of a job keeping the pain in my head from being unbearable, but my swollen ankle was pounding, the brace too tight hours ago.

"Not too close," she said.

It didn't take long for her to find a Best Western that had two adjoining rooms available.

The rooms were clean, colored a generic beige and maroon, and offered a continental breakfast that included make-your-own waffles.

Abbi leaned hard on Hado as he gathered her up from the SUV and led her into one of the rooms. She crawled up on the bed, and if Hado hadn't pulled away the coverlet, she would have been sleeping with no blankets.

She curled up into a ball, head tipped down, and was asleep before Hado had finished tucking her in.

He sat beside her. Then, with a full body shudder, shifted into the big black panther form he preferred. He stretched, extending long claws, and yawned, revealing sharp teeth and a pink tongue. Then he curled around Abbi, eyes half open, watching the locked door.

I eased down onto the foot of the bed in the adjoining room and grunted. "No wonder Abbi fell asleep. Bed's nice. Better than I expected." I stared at my foot, trying to decide if it was worth taking off the brace to shower, or if sleeping with the brace and my pants on was the better idea.

"You can shower first." Lu leaned against the dresser, unbraiding her hair. She had already made sure the locks were set on both doors, and had made it so the door between our rooms stayed open. The blood had gone a long way to heal her, but she was still moving a little more carefully than usual.

"No, you go ahead. It's going to take me a minute to get out of this brace."

She combed her fingers through her hair and scratched at her scalp, the fluid lines of her body arching, as if the braid had been bothering her all day. "I want to linger."

"So? Linger." I waved at the bathroom.

She crossed the floor. Even when she had been a mortal woman and no monsters had changed her blood, she'd been light on her feet, graceful as a dancer.

"Let me." She kneeled and unlaced my boot. I made noises telling her to stop, but she pinned me with a look that I'd learned not to argue with.

After the boot and sock were gone, she worked at the brace. I winced when she tugged. She stilled, her hand on the back of my calf, supporting the weight of my leg.

"Swollen," I said, unnecessarily.

"Let's take it off in the bathroom." She rose and offered her hand. I was not too proud to accept it and lean on her.

The bathroom smelled of soap and pine, and a paper strip across the toilet bowl assured the whole thing had been properly scrubbed.

"Sit." Lu closed the toilet lid and pointed.

"You know I can do this on my own." I maneuvered around her in the small space and took my place on the throne.

"Don't be so stubborn. Just let me…. Brogan, I want to take care of you." She looked up, then back down at me, as if grasping the very last of her patience.

"Sure," I said, catching her hand. "You know I'm all right, don't you?"

She pressed her lips together and nodded.

"Is this about the crash?"

"You…" She pushed her shoulders back, eyes flashing gold. "I hate drinking blood."

It was my time to remain silent.

"When I'm that hungry, I don't think. I miss details. Too much of my head filled with…hunger. I want to know…I need to know you really are okay. I'm missing some time today."

"All right. Let's see. How am I doing?" I gave her a shit-eating grin and made a big deal about leaning back, my hands behind my head, and flexed my biceps for good measure. "Can't say I mind a woman waiting on me hand and foo—ow! The devil, Lula!"

She stood with the ankle brace dangling from one finger, having bent and removed it so quickly I hadn't even seen her move. "You were saying? Woman waiting on you hand and foot?"

I wiped sweat off my forehead and blew out a breath. "I was teasing. You know that, you wicked thing."

She raised an eyebrow.

"It got you out of that mood, didn't it?" I wiped my face again.

She didn't have to take a step to turn on the shower, the room was that small. "What mood?"

"Sad. Worried. I'd say morose, but you've just reminded me how fast you move when you're annoyed." I waggled my eyebrows to take the edge off that comment.

"I wasn't in a mood. I was concerned about you, you oaf."

I heaved up onto my feet. Well, foot. "Lula." I brushed fingers down her arm. "I'm doing good. Good enough. I'm tired, worried about…well, a few things. Worried about you, mostly."

"I'm good." She seemed to hear the echo of my words and added, "and worried too. I feel like we're being led to something. Forced into the hunt. Headwaters, Eunice, Cupid. I don't like it, feeling corralled. But for now, for right now." She slid the shirt she was wearing up and over her head, dropping it to the floor. "I want to get in this water."

She unhooked her bra. Let it fall.

"I want to get into this water with you." Her belt unhooked, then she undid the button and zipper. "So I can touch you. So I can feel you. So I know you're alive and whole and here. And mine."

She slipped out of her underwear, and then, with a fleeting glance over her shoulder—in which I drank in the graceful twist of her spine, the silken white of her skin, made better by the imperfect scattering of freckles —she stepped into the water.

And I was not a man to refuse an invitation from the woman I loved.

"I smell candy." Abbi had woken with the sun, and seemed more her normal self. Enough so, Hado had shifted into his little black house cat shape, and was currently riding on her shoulder as we walked across the street, heading to the Route 66 Junk Hunt, which was held in the Bristow Train Depot and Museum.

"I don't think they'll let a cat into the building," I said.

"Hado's not a cat," she said. "It's bubble gum, isn't it? Do you smell bubble gum?"

"They won't know he's not a cat," I continued. "You could put him in your backpack. They won't notice him there."

I didn't ask why he wasn't in human shape. I'd heard Abbi talking to him this morning before she knew I was awake. I hadn't caught every word, but she'd told him he needed to rest, needed to let her look after them now.

The relationship between her and her shadow was one I didn't fully understand. They weren't the same person, but they were connected so that one really could not, or would not, exist without the other.

In that way, it made sense that each would be the protector over the other.

I understood that. Lu and I were equals, and neither of us dictated our relationship. There was always give and take.

"It will be cute," Abbi said. "People will think a cat

riding on my shoulders is cute." She tugged on my hand to make me look at her. "So cute!" She pulled a face, smile wide and wild, eyes like saucers. "Cuuute."

"I think the backpack is a better idea too," Lu said.

I bumped her shoulder with mine for taking my side on this. "Two against one, Abbi. Looks like we win. Let Hado nap in the backpack."

"What? You win? That's no fair." She tipped her face up, and I was caught by how happy she looked.

I was also caught by how that made me feel. I knew she wasn't what she appeared to be. I knew she wasn't a child. I knew she wasn't *my* child. But seeing her happy, a little bounce in her step, her cheeks rosy, her words breathless and bright, made my heart catch.

She might not be my child, but she was mine, just as much as Lu was mine, as Lorde was mine.

Family. She was family. When had that happened?

"You could have left him back in the SUV with Lorde," Lula said. "They would have been fine curled up and snoring together."

Hado made a tiny kitten chirp, and Abbi grinned widely. "Hado doesn't want to miss out on the fun. Or the candy. You smell it? Bubble gum."

We slowed our pace as we merged with the crowd funneling in toward the event.

The low, warm breeze brought the scent of hot dogs, sweet-salty corn, and fudge. "I can smell a lot of things," I said.

"Candy," Abbi insisted.

"I don't know," I hedged. "Not sure there's candy here. You might be imagining things."

She made a small outraged sound and scowled. "I'm gonna find it and show you."

We'd reached the front of the station and were slowly shuffling forward with everyone else. Lu paid for our entry, and we plunged into the bright light of the building.

It smelled like candy—bubble gum—just like Abbi said, and there was also the rich scents of apple cider, brats, and beer. Just like she said, no one even batted an eye at her walking around with a cat draped over her shoulders.

The space was large, much larger than I'd expected, the ceilings high. Even though the entirety of it was filled with tables and shelves, which were in turn filled with piles of goods, it still echoed enough that voices caught and batted back from odd angles.

A small stage had been set up to the right, where a slender stick of a woman was singing while a burly man played a sweet fiddle.

We had gotten here when the doors opened, but from the number of people already browsing, there had to have been a crowd waiting outside. Probably for hours.

All of that came to me in a glance, the place as familiar as any bazaar, fair, or flea market.

What hit me hard enough to punch air out of my lungs was the overwhelming rush of magic in the place.

It was thick, a song so complex, it was impossible to pick out the individual threads of which it was made. I inhaled, filling my lungs with magic-rich air, magic that coated my mouth, my teeth, my tongue in the flavors of

summer—green and crisp and sweet—and autumn—
smoky and spiced. I shuddered, my whole body shaking
with the experience.

"Brogan." Lu pulled on my hand, drawing me out
of my trance.

How long had I been stuck, standing right in the
middle of the main flow of traffic like a rock that had
tumbled from a cliff? The crowd diverted around me,
but not without several judgmental glances and
comments.

Lu pulled again. I let her guide us out of the
walkway and up to a set of trash cans on a square of
AstroTurf. One can was marked RECYCLE ONLY, with
little drawings of the sorts of things to put in it.

"You feel that?" I asked, all on an exhale.

She frowned and pressed her palm against my
cheek. "Feel what? Is it your head? Are you hurting?"

I took hold of her hand, drawing it away from my
cheek. "I'm fine—I'm not hurting. But I can feel, I can
taste, I can hear—Can't you? Any of those things?—
magic. There's so much magic here."

Lu's eyebrows dipped. She tipped her head as if she
were trying to hear something far away. "Maybe? I can
sense something. You think it's magic?"

I looked around for Abbi. She was on tiptoe in front
of the recycle can, staring into the hole in the top.

"Can you hear it? Abbi? Is the book here?"

"Here?" Abbi turned and stood next to Lu, staring
up at me. "You think so?"

"Maybe not," I said. "But something is here. Something that seems—"

—overwhelming, powerful, haunting—

—"strong. And magical."

"Okay," she said. "Should I try to find it?" She looked up at Lu. "Do you want me to check over by the candy stand? Maybe it's by the bubble gum."

"Can you tell where it's coming from?" Lu held onto Abbi's backpack loop so she wouldn't wander off.

I shook my head. "Everywhere. It's," I turned in a circle as if that would help me get my bearings, "it's everywhere. I think maybe more than one thing?"

"That's possible," Lu said. "You haven't been…" She moved us all to one side as a woman with a double stroller rolled over to dump a McDonald's bag into the trash can. The woman started opening several packets of disposable wipes, which she more or less successfully swabbed over the faces and hands of both squirming kids.

"You haven't been…back all that long," Lu finished. "And we haven't been around magic much."

"I'd argue: the Crossroads, Valentine, Hush, and our rabbit kid? Not to mention the seer and the god? Pretty magic. All of that."

"Our rabbit kid?" Lu asked, and there was something in her voice. Something I liked.

"Well, I know she's not actually a kid…"

"No," Lu's fingers brushed my arm. "I like it, though. As long as Abbi is okay with it."

Abbi shrugged. "I can be your rabbit kid." But her eyes said something more. Something that looked like pure happiness. "For while I'm here, anyway, if you want," she said in a small voice.

Hado meowed.

I cleared my throat, surprised by the emotion. "Good. Yeah, that's good. We want. So can you hear the book, rabbit kid?"

Abbi rocked her head side to side, ear to shoulder, ear to shoulder, once, twice, three times. "There's a lot," she said. "I think there are a lot of things talking here."

"Magic things?" I asked.

Her nose crinkled. "I think so. This way?" She pointed at the candy stand and I almost groaned, but she quickly added, "Not just the candy. I think this way. Really."

She took us deeper into the building. The crowd and competing flows of traffic were too dense to make holding hands easy, and I wasn't moving quickly in the brace, so we settled into a line, Abbi in front, Lu next, and me bringing up the rear.

Abbi was small and bendy and fast. She bolted ahead through a hole in the crowd and was swallowed up by the press of humanity.

"Abbi," Lu called. "Wait." Lu turned her shoulders and squeezed around a family group that was browsing a do-it-yourself metal sign booth, moving in one knot and effectively blocking three quarters of the aisle.

I tried the same move, but there wasn't enough room. When I tried stepping around them on the other side, a man in a wheelchair coming my way took up all the space, and behind him were shoulder-to-shoulder shoppers, some lugging large bags. One was trying to maneuver a half-size windmill vane roughly the size of a compact car between booths.

I lost sight of Lu, I lost sight of Abbi. But it wouldn't be too hard to catch up with them. It was a good bet Abbi would eventually end up at the candy stand.

I waited until there was a break in the foot traffic, then rambled off the way they'd gone, looking for Lu's distinctive red hair, or the bob of Abbi's white. I am a tall man, but even from the advantage of my height, I couldn't see either of them.

They must have continued on down the next aisle. I wove through the crowd, past a booth selling twigs and branches—just cut twigs and branches tied into bundles —for a price that made my eyes water, then one filled with hubcaps, and another with broken window frames and rusted milk jugs.

All of the booths were crowded with people, and lines of customers streamed out from the pay points. I'd thought the "junk" in Junk Hunt was just a play on words, but these people took it seriously, and I heard "farm life" and "cottage cute" and more variations on "eclectic" and "earthy" than I could count.

I finally made it to the end of the aisle and put my back to the wall to scan as much of the room as I could.

Still no Lu. Still no Abbi.

"Brogan?" a man's voice asked.

I knew that voice: Mat Davis.

I took a step, intending to ignore the hell outta the guy, but his hand fell on my shoulder, and he gave me a hearty pat.

"Brogan! It's so good to see you. I like the earring. Is Lula here too? Listen to me. She must be if you are. How wonderful is this to run into you again?"

"Are you following us?"

"What?" His eyebrows shot up, and somehow that expression made him look even more thin and washed out. "Of course not. I'm looking for…well, valuable things." He executed a wink that could be seen from the nosebleed section. "That's why you're here, isn't it?"

I shook my head, but that only brought a smile to his face. "No, don't deny it. You don't have to tell me, but I'll share this with you. I got a tip that there might be some unique items here. Things people will pay large amounts for."

A woman walked by with a LIVE LAUGH LOVE painting that was anything but unique.

Mat chuckled. "Not that everything is going to fit that bill. But I heard," he leaned toward me and lowered his voice, "I heard there might be magical items here. And I know," he leaned back, "I know you don't believe in that stuff, but if you'd just give me a chance to show you that magic is real, I think it would do you a great service. There are collectors who will pay outstanding amounts for something with even a whiff of magic. You and Lula could be set for life."

"We're fine, thanks." I started off to the next aisle.

"There's a book," he said.

It wasn't loud. It didn't have to be because he'd followed me, right up on my heels.

I stopped.

This was foolish, thinking he was talking about the book we were looking for.

There were a lot of books in the world, and many,

many of them contained magic. But Cupid had told us to come to this place.

The seer had told us to come to this place.

Hell, even Headwaters has known there was something here.

I would be a fool to ignore three arrows pointing at the same center.

"All right," I said. "I'll bite. What book?"

His face glowed like I'd just announced my undying friendship. "Oh, I really think you'll like it. It's not like anything I've ever seen. It's this way." He started off, and when he realized I wasn't moving, he stopped.

When had it ever been a good idea to follow Mad Mat Davis anywhere?

Maybe when the one thing we were tasked to find by the god we more or less owed our lives to might be in his possession.

I swore under my breath and closed the distance between us.

"Marvelous!" he crooned. "This is going to knock you on your heels!"

He kept an easy pace and seemed to have no problem threading through the crowd, space opening up as if people unconsciously knew he was coming and moved out of his way.

He said he'd been hunted. He'd said he was long-lived like Lula and me because he'd been attacked.

I didn't know what had attacked him.

I didn't know what he'd been changed into. Was he just a long-lived mortal? Or did he have some powers or abilities, like Lula, like me? Had he really been god-touched like I'd suspected?

Did that make him dangerous or just another bloke trying to make his way down the road?

If he carried a weapon, I couldn't see it on him, and he was wearing close-cut clothes. Difficult to hide much more than a knife.

This could be a trap. My gut said whatever it was, it wasn't on the up and up. But any magical book was rare, and if he'd found the one Cupid was looking for, it was worth following him and buying the thing off of him.

I'd call Lula, but my cell phone hadn't made it out of the crash and we hadn't replaced it yet. I could handle myself. Even with a sore ankle and aching head. Even if he was something not-quite-human, I knew how to hold my own.

I thought he was leading me down to the outer aisle, but he stopped and opened a door at the back of the room. "Short cut," he said as we walked down a service hallway.

Back when this was an active railway station, this had been the way people who worked for the railway got from place to place. We passed doors that might be broom closets, a locker room, bathroom, and finally, a storage room.

Document boxes were stacked on shelves, and the shelves took up all the walls. Six small roll-top desks—the sort that should be in a library—filled the center space.

"Here," he said, his voice warm with excitement. "I asked if I could store it here until the show was over. I didn't dare leave it in my vehicle, and I wasn't done shopping yet. Sit. Yes, right there is fine, fine."

I didn't want to sit, but he was already at the shelf opening the lids of several boxes. I dragged a chair away from a desk and positioned it so I could see him and the door we came through—the only entry or exit of the room.

"I know it's here. Don't worry. This is…Hold on, I think…They wrote my name on the box. How thoughtful." He pushed the lid aside and carried the box to the desk nearest him. "I do hope you'll be careful with this. And remember, I found it, but I'm willing to negotiate a price to get you started in the supernatural trade."

He lifted a cloth-wrapped rectangular item out of the box. It appeared to be the size and shape of a book, but I didn't feel any change in magic that indicated it was the book I wanted.

He closed the distance between us and placed the wrapped book on the desk to my left.

"Go ahead," he said with birthday-party glee. "Open it. I can't wait for you to see this."

I flipped one edge of the cloth off to the right, the other edge off to the left.

Magic wasn't any stronger, wasn't any louder. I didn't hear the universe singing.

But there was no doubt at all that the book was indeed the spell book of the gods.

CHAPTER TEN

"You can tell, can't you?" Mad Mat asked. "It's old —it's obviously old. But the magic. You can see that it's magic. Real as can be."

It was more than magic, it was pages and pages of spells written by hundreds of gods. Experimental, one-of-a-kind spells. It was dangerous. It was powerful. I couldn't believe he'd found it.

"Did you buy it here? That was fast." I hadn't touched it. I remembered the first time I touched it, I'd been in spirit form and it had knocked me on my ass.

"I had a lead. So I arrived last night and got in line before sunrise. Once I stepped into the building, I was drawn to it." His voice went dreamy. "I could hear it calling me. Well, not with an actual voice. I believe in magic. I'm not experiencing auditory hallucinations."

This was making his day, and he was bursting with pride. "Go on, Brogan. Go ahead. You can touch it."

"Have you touched it?" I asked.

"You just saw me carry it over here. Weren't you

paying attention? I should have shown it to Lula instead. She's here, isn't she? She'd appreciate it. She'd believe it's magic."

"Did you open it?" I pressed.

He frowned. "Well, no. There's a lock on it. The seller said they didn't have the key. And I don't want to damage it. Of course, before I sell it, I'll hire an expert to carefully pick the lock."

"You held it without the cloth over it?"

He blew out a breath and leaned forward. "I cannot believe you are so dense. Here." He lifted the book out of the cloth, bare fingers on the cover, no cloth shielding him, although there was a blur of power, a swift glow that lit beneath his fingers. "Do you believe me now? I touched it, I am touching it. I don't know why you're so worried about that. It's magic, not poison. Here."

He tossed the book at me. The act startled me, and I reacted without thinking. I caught the book in one hand.

Magic hit me like a tsunami wave. I drowned in it, unbreathing, the underwater sensation of weightlessness while being dragged beneath the ever-growing pressure, a punishing agony. It wasn't a lightning strike of power hitting me like last time.

It was consumption.

And I was the meal.

"Now do you believe me?" Mad Mat asked, his voice coming from over my head, under my feet, everywhere around me, and inside my mind. "Play me the fool, Brogan Gauge, but I see what you are. Unfortunately for you, you are extremely *useful*.

"In the right circumstance, you are the key to what I desire."

He stood, or maybe had already been standing, but now he was taller, larger, filling the room and staring down at me from somewhere far above the glistening waterline.

"But not like this. No, you can't be my key like this. That's what I have Lula for. You, Brogan, only become useful to me one way." He drew a weapon from behind his back. Something magic, something sharp.

"The only way you're useful is dead." He chanted three words and struck.

The weapon plunged through the air, across a great distance, piercing through the deep, deep water. It should be slow. The water should dull the strike, but the weapon plunged fast and true.

Pain shattered my chest, stabbed my heart, burning hot, then freezing cold.

This was what it felt like to be harpooned.

My heart beat too fast, panicked, and then it slowed.

The world went soft. My vision closed in. Gently, the darkness fell.

I inhaled, and that was soft too, velvet filling me, smothering, comforting.

I remembered Lula, her smile, her eyes, her laughter, her sorrow. I wanted to tell her one more time that I loved her, but couldn't sort out the words.

I'm sorry…

And then I was gone.

. . .

THE FOG WAS ROSE-COLORED. I hadn't expected that. Fog, yes. But that blush, like a sunrise, like a sunset, draped over tropical water.

It glittered. That was the best word. It glittered.

I wanted it. Wanted to feel that soft sunlight.

I walked toward it.

"This," a low melodious male voice said, "is an interesting choice."

I was alone. I had to be alone. Just me and the sunset. The sunrise. An end and beginning together.

"A man such as you…" the voice went on, and maybe it wasn't melodious. Maybe it was dry, observant, but with something beneath all that, a keen sense of curiosity lending it texture. "…has the very rare chance to make other, interesting choices."

I stopped. The light hadn't drawn any closer, and I was sure I'd been walking for…time. For something that felt like time, but the measurements of it slipped, dream-like, away from me.

"Do you know who I am?" the voice asked.

I didn't want to look away from the warmth, the light. It was dimmer now; the rose was losing its depth. It wouldn't shine forever, was already fading.

"Do you wish to know who I am? I find curiosity to be one of the more enduring traits of humans. Not that you have been among them as long as you may have wanted to be. You and Lula."

The name, *her* name, wrapped around me like a chorus of voices, a garden of fragrance, a universe of stars. Lula. My heart. My love.

"Yes," the voice said. "Love. Such a simple word for

something which contains so much power. The power to comfort. The power to heal. The power to lift a soul and call it home. Where is your home, Brogan Gauge? Do you remember it?"

The curiosity in those words made me turn, made me look away from the glitter to answer the voice.

It was not a voice. Not *just* a voice. It was a god.

He was tall and very lean. His dark hair was combed back as if it were a daily observance of perfection, his eyes deep enough to swallow the void. All the lines of him seemed whittled to a razor's edge.

The wooden staff—no, snath—supported the curved blade of a great scythe over his head, the weapon dripping with black and silver blood.

"Who?" I spoke, without air to carry the word.

"Death," he said, with a slight nod. "Thanatos, if you wish. Do you know of me?"

I did. What I knew of him was fear. He was the monster I raged against, the angel I prayed to.

"Death," I said.

"Yes," he agreed. "Do you remember me?"

I remembered he was the god who had abandoned me. Abandoned Lu. The god who had trapped us in a state of un-living. Both of us not quite dead, nor fully alive for nearly a hundred years.

I hated him. Feared him. Longed for him. I never wanted to meet him. Not without Lula by my side.

"You don't look like Death." There was something strange about him. The scythe made sense, his sharp, emaciated features, bones nearly visible beneath his skin. The eyes of eternal darkness. But something was wrong.

"Do I not?" he encouraged.

It was his shirt. That's what was wrong. He should be wearing a cloak, tatters, funerary ash.

Instead, he wore a bright red T-shirt with the map of a town, or maybe the shape of a state, drawn on it. Letters above the map said: ORDINARY IS NEVER BORING and below the map: ASK ME FOR A TOUR.

There were little waves on one side—an ocean, I thought—and tourist destinations drawn out, including one that appeared to be a shrine to a penguin.

"Are you really Death? The god of death?"

"Of course," he said, looking pleased to be recognized. "However, my attention and attire are occasionally turned toward things other than ending mortal suffering."

I didn't know what to say to that.

"Vacationing," he said, as if I should have guessed that's what he was talking about. We were walking again, his tone conversational. "Have you heard of such?"

"Vacation?" I asked.

"Just."

"Yes," I said. "Most people have heard of vacations. Holiday. Leave."

"I find it…interesting."

"Vacations?"

He hummed. "A god can take a day off, a month, a millennium. Time away from the weight and responsibility of his power."

"Are you taking time away?" My thoughts snail crawled, while the sunset light slipped away. Soft gray twilight surrounded us, shot through with glints of silver going gold.

"Yes, I am. Vacationing," he added, in case I wasn't following along. "There are rules to such a thing."

I waited for him to explain. When it felt like time had stretched too far, I asked: "Am I a part of those rules?"

He made a considering sound. "No. But you may be a reason I bend them. I am a very old god, Brogan Gauge. Older than a great many of the gods. I am one of the *originals*."

He said that last word as if it chopped more wood and carried more water than other words.

"I was there at the creation. I will be there standing at the end. My perspective reaches across all existence, beyond, and beyond even that. It affords me things other gods may not possess."

"I don't understand."

"There are rules that cannot be broken, and there are rules that only I, or one such as I, can bend enough that I can appear to be here, on your dreaming, on your death, even though I am at my leisure, vacationing."

The gold lights were growing, warming.

"But why? Why come to me now?"

"So that we may have this conversation. You interest me."

We strolled through the silver and gray and gold, silent awhile. My thoughts gathered, slowly, but not as slowly as before.

"You only noticed me because I've been not-dead for so long."

"Not entirely true. There are many souls who spend their lives not-dead. There are many creatures and beings who breathe through an endless count of days, yet never live them. You interest me for what you are, Brogan Gauge. What you can be."

"What can I be?"

"In the hands of some, a weapon. In the hands of others, a balm."

"What does that mean?"

"There are those who would use you. Use you and Lula. Not for the thing that you have become—not-dead, as you called it—but for what you have always been: a lightning rod for god power."

Even in this nowhere state, his words zinged through me, like fire finding oxygen.

"You can sense god power, and there will be a day when you use god power. Because of this, you were targeted, found, attacked." He inclined his head. "You wandered and were found again."

"By a god," I said, catching on. A memory flashed, wings, a galaxy turning, biker boots and tattoos. "Cupid found us. And…and now I'm dead."

"You are very much not dead," he said, offended. "Nor will you become so until I have decided thus."

"But this isn't living. I'm not alive. Is this a…a dream?"

"Think of it as a pause." He extended his long, boney finger and pressed an imaginary button. "If we ring the bell, will the doorway to death open?" He curved his hand at his ear as if listening. "No. No one is home. No one to let you in. Ah, well. A pity." From the gleam in his eye, this situation was delighting him.

"Life has her powers," Death said, "and I have mine. You will not die until your death agrees with me." He leaned toward me until his mouth was a breath away from my ear and whispered, "Today, your death does not agree with me."

Every inch of my spirit, soul, body, whatever I was, froze and shivered.

"Does Cupid want me dead?"

Death pulled back and stood in front of me. "Cupid is, all things considered, wholly *adequate* as a god."

He made it sound like a grand compliment. Maybe from him it was.

"He has, in most ways, shown you kindness. There is another who has known you, seen you, damaged you. A god who would have been your undoing. If," he added with a nod, "I hadn't found you interesting."

"Which god? How will I know? How can I keep Lula safe?"

"She goes by many names and many faces. She has been there, beside you, a lifetime ago. She has watched you, hungered for your bones. She sent you here. You already know her, Brogan Gauge, and by her appearance as Mat Davis."

Lightning again, a blast, hard enough to rock me off my foundation.

"Mad Mat, Mat Davis is a god?"

"An illusion a god wears, yes."

"He...*she* sent those creatures, those monsters who attacked us all those years ago?"

"Yes."

"Why? Because I can sense god power? Not very damn good at it if I didn't sense it in the god who wanted us dead."

"She does not want you dead. You are useful to her as a tethered spirit. Lula is useful to her as a *thrawn*. If she had wanted you dead that first time, years ago, you would be so."

"But now?" My thoughts juttered, still shaking from this revelation. Too many memories rising sharp and hot, too much anger for any of it to make sense, for any one thing except rage to lift above the roar.

I was mad as hell.

"She wanted the book to send me here. Tricked me into touching it."

"Yes. You would once again be a tethered spirit. Bound to Lula. Bound to the old road."

As he said it, the gold light grew and grew and rose into the sky, until there was no silver twilight. There was only the road beneath us, concrete, sun-baked and faded, the sky watered down to a dusty blue. I could not feel the ground, could not hear the soles of my boot and brace falling on the road as we walked.

This might be the real world, the solid world. But I was not solid within it.

Tethered spirit once again.

"I will not give you a choice in this, Brogan Gauge. There are too many knots and too many strings attached to your fate. And so, this will not be of your free will, but of mine."

He stopped, and I found I couldn't take another

step. He appeared in front of me again, skin a thin wax spread over bone, endless blackness filling his eyes.

He was terrifying, but the tourist trap T-shirt distracted a bit.

"Give me the weapon you carry."

It took a moment to understand what he was asking for. "The letter opener?"

"The dagger of Carnwennan is not a letter opener, just as Excalibur is not a toothpick. This dagger can injure gods, as very few earthly weapons can."

He stuck out his hand, palm up, and crooked two fingers in a "gimme" motion.

I twisted my hand back to my waistband, where I'd last put the dagger. I didn't expect it to be there because I was not really alive, not really physical, and therefore a physical letter opener—dagger—should not have hitched a ride to this spirit space.

My hand closed around the white hilt. I drew it and settled it onto Death's palm.

"Exactly." He ran his finger along the edge. He didn't bleed, the nick from the dagger so shallow, it was more like a paper cut.

The dagger pulsed, gold, silver, copper, black, then gold again.

"Before it would have injured a god," he said. "Now, it will undo a god." His voice dropped into a low growl. "Delightful."

He tossed the dagger to me. I fumbled it twice before catching it. It didn't feel any different.

"Since I am on vacation," he said, his voice back to its normal timbre, "this death, *your* death, would require my direct attention. I find I do not wish to cancel my vacation early to guide your soul beyond this place of rest. Therefore…"

He leaned toward me and bent at the waist, a tower of force, of infinite power. A god and more than a god. Older than a god. *Original.*

"Therefore," he repeated, "I deny your current condition. I am not life, but I do not grant you death." He straightened. "Return, soul. Return to living. Return, spirit. Return to life. Breathe and live and love. Fulfill your destiny among the living, the unalive, the gods and deities, all."

He drew his scythe forward, planting the wooden snath into the ground in front of him. I expected him to strike me, but the weapon morphed so that the snath became a string, and the arched blade turned into a bright yellow kite.

There was no breeze I could feel, but the kite rose into the air.

"What are you doing?" I asked.

"It is a Delta kite," he said, as if that was the important thing I needed to know. "It is excellent in uncertain winds. Easy for beginners. Hold the line. Yes. Exactly. And the reel. There. Adequate. Now. Return. And *remember.*"

A wind kicked, swirling and rolling like ocean currents, bringing with it the smell of fir trees, salt air, and summer rain on hot pavement. The kite jerked, buffeted by the wind. I corrected it, my hands automatically trying to steady the little yellow wing's swoop and tremble.

The wind grew stronger; the kite soared higher and higher, until the reel was nearly empty of line. I tugged, trying to bring the kite down, closer to the ground, away from the wild storm building.

The kite stuttered and dove.

I reeled in the line, but couldn't wind the string fast enough. Childhood reflexes kicked in. I ran, trying to keep tension between me and the kite, trying to keep it flying.

One step, two, three—

—and my boot hit pavement, smooth and black. Momentum kept me running, my lungs working like I was coming down out of a sprint. I inhaled the scent of oak leaves and grass, and beyond that, a thicker blend of automobile oil, rust, and strangely, caramel.

I put the brakes on and blinked hard. The kite was gone, Death was gone.

The pain radiating from my ankle, cramping in my calves and shoulders, and the pounding of my heart and head indicated that yes, I was uncomfortably alive.

I had no idea where I was.

The road was actually a drive, almost too narrow for a car. A farmhouse sat half an acre off at the end of the drive. The house had two stories, with dormers above and a porch below. It needed a new paint job, but otherwise seemed sturdy enough.

Behind me was a barn big enough for two stalls, split wood fencing edging the field. When the breeze shifted, I got a noseful of the distinct smell of chickens.

"Hey!" a woman's voice called out.

I squinted at the figure waving her hand on the farmhouse porch.

"You're late!"

I, stupidly, looked behind me, as if there were someone else she was waving at.

"You, Brogan. I'm talking to you."

"Eunice?"

Her cackle was all I needed to know I'd guessed right.

Then a familiar bark filled the air and Lorde, our big fluffy dog, barreled out of the house and down the road toward me. I still had the dagger in my hand and quickly stowed it into my waistband.

I knelt and got an armful of wriggling, whining, happy, licking dog.

"Hey, girl," I said, burying my face in her fur and breathing in her familiar smell. "Hey, sweet girl. Is Lu here too? And Abbi?"

Lorde stopped wiggling and let me lean on her, her soft panting the sound of home.

"Get on up here," Eunice called. "You have made a mess of things. We need to iron it all out."

Wings whispered above my head, and I glanced up to the sky. An owl continued onward, flying ahead of me toward the house, just in case I was too dense to know which way I should be walking.

I straightened. Lorde circled me twice, whining and licking my fingers as she came to a stop at my left. "Is Lu here, girl?"

Lorde whined again, and I knew Lula was not here.

I glanced behind me. I could leave. Once I figured out what state I was in, I could hitch a ride.

A flash of silver, curved like a scythe, burned briefly through the air and was gone, leaving only blue sky behind.

Death had sent me here. He and his kite. There must be a reason why. A reason that would lead me to Lula. I got moving, following the owl to the farmhouse, Lorde at my side.

CHAPTER ELEVEN

"Tell me all of it." Eunice paced between the kitchen sink and the teakettle. She kept reaching up, half opening a cupboard, then pressing it closed again. "Tell me everything you remember."

She stopped at the kettle, turned to where I sat at the kitchen table and deposited a huge mug into my hands.

The steam smelled of lemons, chamomile, and rose hips. I thought I could drink for a year and not kill my thirst. I raised the mug, but my hands shook so badly, tea slopped over the edge and onto my fingers.

"Oh, I see." She took the mug back and gave me a warm, damp washcloth I ran over my fingers, then wearily over my face.

The warm cloth smelled of tea, and I closed my eyes, welcoming the moment of relief.

I felt like I'd been hit by a truck. Everything ached from my ass to my teeth. I wanted to linger in the darkness, breathing the scent of tea for a decade. Maybe two.

Under the table, Lorde draped over my feet, her breathing anchoring me. Eunice had contacted Lawrence to pick her up at the Junk Hunt and bring her out here. Lula and Abbi had not been found.

"Try this." Eunice took the cloth. I was too tired to fight for it. I blinked against the light that seem bright enough to burn, but barely cast any shadows.

A migraine, I thought. This was what a migraine felt like. Or an aneurysm.

Or death.

Lorde whined softly.

No, not death. I might never know what death felt like if the gods had their way.

"Brogan, drink some tea." Eunice's voice was gentle, sweet with melody, slipping through the car crash in my brain.

I blinked until the room unfuzzed, then took the smaller, sturdy tea cup she offered me. It was about a quarter of what she'd given me before, the handle and weight of it manageable, even in my unsteady hands.

This time I got tea to my mouth and swallowed. The taste was a miracle.

I drank it as quickly as I could, only registering it was lukewarm after I'd drained it down.

"How's the pain?" She exchanged my empty cup for an identical full one. I drained it, too.

"Not worse," I said with a chainsaw voice. I cleared my throat, and she offered another cup. She also pressed two pills into my other hand.

"Aspirin, nothing fancy," she said. "It should help."

I squinted at the round white pills, decided they

looked enough like aspirin that I wasn't going to turn them away, and swallowed them down with more tea.

By the fourth cup, I was feeling more human.

After the slice of toast slathered in apple butter, I could think again.

And what I thought was that I needed to find Lula.

"…better if I know now. That way I can tell you which way…" Eunice was leaning against the oven, a big mug in her hand, the smell of cocoa in the air.

"Ah," she said, her gaze locking on me. "There you are. I wondered how long it'd be until you came back. Almost took myself to bed, figuring it would be morning before your brain fully connected."

"I—what time is it? What…what day is it? Year?" The last word came out as a punched whisper, panic wrapping fingers around my throat and squeezing.

Lorde moved and plunked her big head into my lap. My hand dropped automatically to pet her.

"It's been one week since I saw you last. It is almost midnight. You are at my house outside of Geary, Oklahoma."

I stacked and restacked that information, hoping it would take me back to understanding what the hell had happened to me.

"You've had half a pot of tea, two pieces of bread, and two aspirins. You've been here about six hours now, and I'm happy to say you're no longer catatonic. Let's talk. What happened?"

"I thought… Shouldn't you know?"

"I know what might have been, what probably was, but I didn't follow you to see what decisions you made.

It's always better for me to hear it out loud. Did all the things I told you were going to happen come true?"

"I don't…I don't remember what you said."

"Did you touch the book?"

"Yes."

"Did a god betray you?"

"Yes."

"Did Death his damned self come for your soul?"

I scowled. "Yes."

"Well, there you have it. I was right. About everything. Why don't people listen to old women? Am I invisible over here? Like I can't see the damn futures."

"You also…you said it would break Lula's heart."

She lowered into the chair across from me, her back to the door. "When you find her, you'll see I got that right too," she said, not unkindly. "Tell me your story, Brogan Gauge. Let me hear what future you're headed to."

So I went over it, starting at our meeting with Cupid, call to Headwaters, and then finally, the Junk Hunt, Mad Mat, and the book. By then I was slurring my words, exhaustion catching up with me. She handed me a cup of coffee and a slice of spice cake and I finished the rest of the story about Death between bites of pecan and maple frosting.

"Now that I've told you everything, I need to know what you wanted us to find for you. Maybe it fits into all this."

She turned her empty cup on the table between her hands. "It is a reed. It sounds inconsequential when I say it like that. The reed is a mouthpiece, a focal, a manifestation of my power. It was taken from me, from us, from the muse I am. It leaves us, me, vulnerable, unable to hear all the notes of destiny."

"Stolen, not lost?"

"Stolen. A god. The one who hides as another. Mad Mat used it to find and to see possibilities. To find you. To press on the scale of the future and bend destiny."

I rubbed my hand over my face, tired. "What does it look like? A stick? A piece of grass? A cane?"

"It's a reed. It is used in the mouthpiece of musical instruments. Clarinet, bagpipe, shehnai, harmonica…"

"Trombone?" Mad Mat had been carrying a trombone when he'd found us in that gazebo in Galena. He'd kept forgetting he was holding it, but had been reluctant to set it down. If it was part of a muse's power, if it had something to do with seeing the future, or futures, and influencing them, then it was a powerful item indeed.

"It could fit a trombone, though you'd never get a sweet tune out of it." She stood and returned to the same cupboard, opening it, and shutting it again. "You've seen it, haven't you?"

"I think so." I leaned back in the chair, and the joints creaked and popped. "Mad Mat was carrying an instrument, a trombone. That might be it."

She moved away from the counter, every line of her tense. A faint echo of how I'd seen her before—all the versions of her—flipped through her like shadowed notes written behind flame.

"Help me, Brogan Gauge, and I will help you."

She was a part of this, tangled in this knot of gods

and magic along with Lula and me. There was only one answer left. "Yes."

She released a long breath. Maybe she had seen other answers in my future, but I knew I'd chosen right.

"Then this is how I can help you," she said. "When you have to choose, choose the reed. If you don't…" She worked her mouth, but no sound came out. She raised her elbow and coughed into it. "Well, that can't be said. Not by me. But trust me on this. You must choose the reed." She jerked her head, gaze on the door.

Lorde stood, facing the door, too, her ears tall, her tail curled high over her back. She *woof*ed low and softly whined.

Emotion flickered over Eunice's round features before she relaxed. "Good," she whispered.

The knock was hesitant. I couldn't imagine Cupid, or any god, knocking like that.

Just the same, I stood and quickly braced one hand on the table to stay standing.

Lorde's tail gave an experimental wag.

"Yes, yes," Eunice said louder. "Come on in. We were waiting for you."

The door opened. I caught an impression of white hair and big eyes and a black panther, then all that was a blur because Abbi was running toward me, chattering. "I fell for you. I fell for you. And I found you. I knew I'd find you if I went back to the moon, and I did. I did."

Her arms were around me, squeezing tight. I almost toppled under the force of her, but the big panther padded up behind me and leaned, holding me in place.

I closed my eyes and breathed to hold back the unexpected tears of relief. I patted her back gently.

"It's okay," I said. "It's going to be okay. Are you all right? Are you hurt? Abbi, oh, now, pumpkin, why are you crying?"

She snuffled, and it was wet with tears. She tipped her head up. "Pumpkin. I like that." Her smile went watery, and the tears made tracks down her cheeks. "I thought you died, then I thought you were lost. And you were and Lula too, and everyone was gone and you were lost, weren't you?"

"Yeah. Yes, I was."

"I couldn't see you, but I remembered the owl lady said I fell for you, so I went to the sky, back to the moon, and I saw you here. I found you." Her smile was a little steadier this time. "I found you."

I wiped tears off her cheek. "Yes, you did. Nicely done."

The cupboard opened again. Eunice withdrew a pack of bright pink desserts of roughly the same size and shape as a snowball.

"Would you like a snowball?" she asked.

I nodded at Abbi, who still hadn't released me.

"Is it a cookie?" Abbi asked.

"Not quite," Eunice said.

"Is it a moonball?"

"It has marshmallow in it."

"It's okay," I told her.

Abbi released me, but only enough so she could see Eunice.

"They look like bubble gum," Abbi said. "I like that.

I like marshmallow too. How did you know I fell to find him? Because you're a muse?" She held out her hand and Eunice passed her the package. Abbi leaned back against me and tore it open.

"I can hear the music of tomorrow," Eunice said. "It sings me the futures."

"Neat," Abbi said through a mouth of marshmallow.

"Do you know where Lula is?" I asked.

Eunice tipped her head, but Abbi said, "I know where she is."

My knees almost buckled, the relief was so great. Hado leaned again, propping me up.

"Where?" I asked. "Where is she?"

"He took her," Abbi said.

"Who took her?" I asked.

"That god."

"Cupid," I said before automatically correcting, "Mad Mat. Is that the god who took her?"

Abbi nodded. "I thought he was old, but I was wrong. He was pretending to be old. He's a god, but doesn't look like what he should look like."

"Illusion, trickery, chaos," Eunice said.

"Where is he?" I asked, moving toward the door, but realizing I didn't have resources. No phone, no car, no direction. Not even a damn plan.

"I could show you. We can drive. Oh," she wiped fingers on her bright skirt. "We broke the truck and left the other car, didn't we?"

"I'll call a taxi. A Lyft. Do you have a phone?" I

turned to Eunice and caught the keys flying toward my face.

"Truck's out back." She pulled a duffle out from a low cupboard. "Blankets, some food, water. Things I thought you might need."

I swallowed, the flood of relief, of gratitude washing against the shores of my reserve. "Thank you. For helping me."

Abbi made a little sound.

"For helping us," I said.

"Hold true to our deal," Eunice warned. "Remember what I said. I promise you, Brogan Gauge, if you betray me, worse, if you don't follow through and bring the reed to me, you will regret that decision for the rest of your life."

"I understand." I didn't have to tell her I was going to find Lu first. That one thing—Lula's safety—would always come before any promises to gods, muses, or monsters.

Eunice was a muse who could hear the music of starlight, the songs of tomorrows. I figured she could hum my future better than I could.

"You'll need a phone." She gave me one from her pocket. "And you need to hear this: Cupid gave you a dime. All of you. It is as real as any other thing."

I waited to see if she was going to make sense of that, but she chuckled softly and patted the halo of her hair, bracelets clicking. "Go on. That's enough. Time is pouring out. Don't waste it."

I bent for the duffle, but Abbi had already scooped it

up and was wrestling the strap over her shoulder and backpack. "Shotgun," she said.

"There isn't anyone else who can ride in the passenger seat," I said.

"There's Lorde. And Hado." She strolled through the door into the night, navigating the porch and stairs as if it were bright as day.

Hado meowed, a little kitten sound, and bounded after Abbi in his small cat form.

"Yes, you would," she said to her shadow. "You like sitting up front."

Lorde stretched and yawned, then trotted up next to me. She tipped her big fuzzy head, her dark eyes soft and curious.

"Lula," I said. "We're going to go find Lula, girl."

Lorde's tail wagged, and she opened her mouth briefly, then nudged my hand.

"I know, I know," I said. "Time to go." I glanced back at the muse.

She leaned against the counter, an hourglass in her hand. She raised an eyebrow, then tipped it over. "Quickly."

I didn't have to be told twice.

WHAT PAINT REMAINED on the truck appeared to have been yellow at one time. That was the best thing I could say about the vehicle, other than none of tires were flat.

The windshield was cracked, the dash ripped half out, the ignition hanging by the wires.

A stiff brown horse blanket that still smelled like

horse sweat covered the bottom and back of the bench seat. The engine, when it caught, brayed like a donkey with a chronic smoking habit.

"Can you go faster?" Abbi asked, or I think that's what she shouted over the rock-crushing growl of the engine.

I shook my head. The gas pedal was on the floor. We were going maybe forty-five miles an hour, tops, slowing on every hill we climbed.

The road was unlit, and while the truck had two functioning headlights, one was cocked to the side of the road, illuminating the grassy shoulder and doing nothing to make the road itself easier to see.

"How close?" I yelled.

We'd been on the road for almost two hours, more or less following the Canadian River southward. Lorde was curled with her tail over her nose, Hado on Abbi's lap.

Abbi had her hands clapped over her ears, but her gaze was intent on the road ahead. "That way!" She dropped one hand to point to the left, then slapped it over her ear again.

I flipped on the blinkers out of habit—I wasn't even sure the things worked—and took the turn.

This road was smoother, and led us through three intersections, all quiet at this time of night. There was no traffic. Somewhere in the back of my throbbing head, I wondered if the truck was loud enough to bring the local law enforcement out for a look.

"There." Abbi pointed.

I followed her finger as she sent us through what

might have been a downtown area, except the only buildings were a car repair shop and a brick building with boarded windows.

Beyond that fleeting glance of civilization spooled out a country road, which we followed until Abbi grabbed my arm and held on. "Here," she said, "here, here, here."

I stepped on the brakes and overshot the driveway by half a block. Abbi twisted in the seat, peering out the back window at the dark drive.

"Here?" I asked. I didn't know how she heard me, but she nodded. I goosed the truck closer to the side of the road and killed the engine.

The silence dropped so suddenly, it was like we'd stepped through a hatch and into deep space.

Darkness was a force, a texture, cool and slick, impossible to push away, thick enough I wanted to gulp air and swim through it.

"There's a house up there," Abbi said, her voice a normal volume, but slightly muffled by my blown hearing. "He's in that house."

"Lula too?"

She nodded.

"You stay here."

She leaned back so she could look at me. "I go with you."

"Abbi."

"I've got powers. You know I do. You've seen them. I'm strong. I go with you."

"There's a god in there," I said. "A god who almost..." I swallowed, pushing away an experience I hadn't even processed yet. "Almost killed me. If you go with me, I will not do my best. Be my best."

Not with you there, I thought. *Not if I'm worried about keeping you safe, making sure I don't lose you too.*

"That's okay," she said. "I'll look after you."

"That's not. I'm not worried about…"

Abbi yanked the door handle and shouldered the door open. She hopped out, Hado trotting beside her.

"Damn it." I grabbed the duffle and pushed out the driver's side. Lorde was with me, silent as the night, no longer just a happy dog, but a formidable hunter.

I should tell her to stay behind too. The memory of her jumping between Lula and the Hunter's gun flashed through me, making my breath stutter.

I snapped my fingers so softly I couldn't hear it. Lorde came to heel, moving with me as if we'd been doing this for years.

And in a way, we had been. Even when I was in spirit form, she'd been able to see me and understand me.

Abbi jogged ahead of us, her white hair trackable even in this darkness. She moved quietly and quickly. Hado must have been beside her, but was invisible. She paused at the mouth of the driveway, waiting for me to catch up.

"You need to wait behind—"

"Do you think we should use our coins?"

"What?"

"The Cupid dimes. Should we call him? Would he fight that Mat god?"

Maybe. It wasn't a bad idea. Cupid had given us the

dimes to call him if we needed him. He said he'd know if we were trying to reach him. I stuck my hand into my front pocket where I'd left the dime.

"Or do you think the Mat god would hear the dime too?" Abbi asked.

I held very still and blew out a breath. My head was still pounding, from the injury, from being rejected by death, from losing a week's time. Whatever healing magic was in the earring, I was pretty sure I'd tapped it out.

But before I took another step, I needed to be a lot smarter. I needed to think through my actions.

I didn't want to tip off the other god. Not yet.

"We'll call him as soon as we find Lula," I said. "Until then, don't use the dime."

"Is this a plan? Did we make a plan? We're so good at this."

I crouched and opened the duffle. There was a med kit, which I pushed aside, a blanket, an entire tub of wet wipes. Rope, wire that looked like it'd been in the duffle for a few seasons, and the harmonica Lu had taken from the storage unit.

I didn't know how Eunice had gotten a hold of it, but having to deal with three gods in two days made me not care to work out the details. It was magic. I was glad it had been returned to us, safe. Just as I intended for Lu to return to me, safe.

"Why do you have a dagger in your belt?" Abbi asked. "Is it magic? Will it stab a god?"

"It will stab a god." I dug through the remaining items Eunice had packed. A change of one-size-fits-all sweatshirt and sweatpants, an adjustable wrench, a hammer, a bag of pretzels, and a box of cookies.

In the corner was a small wooden box that hummed with magic. I used the sleeve of the sweatshirt to pick it up. Polished a deep brown with streaks of ruby and gold, it had a simple brass clasp.

I took a breath and opened it.

The scent of cedar reached me. It was empty. Open, it appeared to be nothing more than a box. I closed it again. Definitely magic.

"The god will know we're coming. He's been tracking me, us, too long not to expect this," I said. "You should stay out here, Abbi. So you can call for help once I find Lula."

"Mat god doesn't know we're here," she said.

"Gods know where I am, apparently, alive or dead."

She shook her head. "We're in my shadow. It's too dark for gods to see through. I can do this for us. So we can find Lula together. We're a team."

Her eyes, in this darkness, in her darkness, glittered silver. I was reminded she had powers the gods did not rule.

Everything in me wanted to wrap her up in a blanket and hide her away out here, where I knew she wouldn't be hurt. But I needed every awvantage I could get.

I shoved the duffle under some scrub brush. I might need some items, but lugging it around in the house would hamper my movements.

"I hate this," I said, staring at the house. "Taking

you in there, risking… You could get hurt. I don't want to… You could get lost."

"It's gonna be okay." Abbi took my hand, and the warm strength of her conviction, of her power trickled into me.

"Why bring her here? Why would a god hide here in Oklahoma when the universe is their playground?"

Abbi shrugged. "You're here. Lula's here. I think that's what Mat God wants. You."

"And Lula," I said.

"Mat God has her."

"Not for long. When we find her, you're going to grab her and run as fast as you can."

"Oh, yeah. Sure. Run away."

"With Lula."

"I'm good at running. Really good. But she doesn't really do that. Run away."

"You're going to make her do it. You're strong. You have power. Hado can carry her. You can make her run away."

She scrunched up her face. "I'll try."

"Good. Let's go find a god."

I MOVED TOWARD THE HOUSE, crouched low so as not to draw any attention. Abbi rolled her eyes and headed to the house like she was strolling down the lane for ice cream.

Lorde moved with me, tuned into my distress and the danger ahead.

Thoughts rolled through my mind on repeat. *What if*

Lula's hurt? What if she's being tortured? And the worst: *what if she's dead?*

I'd know. I'd know if she were dead. I spared a breath to pray Death wouldn't answer his door for her soul.

Abbi paused in front of the postage stamp of a porch on the postage stamp of a house. It was a ranch-style home, painted something lighter than the night—tan maybe—with asphalt roofing and sagging gutters that needed the leaves dumped out of them.

The night was darker than night, and the wind was quiet in the surrounding crabapple trees. I should have noticed how hot it was, because summer nights like this, with clouds squatting the sky, were always humid in Oklahoma. But I didn't feel the night's heat. Didn't feel the heavy air.

Abbi's power, Abbi's shadow, kept the world at arm's length.

"Do we go in this way?" She pointed at the front door. It looked like any other front door. Nothing magic. Nothing unusual.

"Let's walk around." We made our way through dry grass, almost hip-high, flattening a path as we went. A split-wood fence separated the yard from an old orchard. From the dense, overgrown weeds, this place hadn't been tended in years.

Even so, there was something almost too perfect about how it was overgrown. As if an artist had drawn this land and added things: a fallen log with a hillock rising next to it; a fence post leaning just so with a small bird's nest balancing on top; a patch of Queen Anne's Lace catching moonlight.

It looked charming and harmless.

It felt fake and dangerous.

This place was an illusion, a hood hiding the cobra's fangs.

"How long will your shadow hide us?" I asked Abbi.

"All night. Day is harder."

"Remember what I said?" I pulled the dagger out of my belt and slipped it up my sleeve. I rolled my wrist, making sure to seat it safely against my bare skin.

"Run away with Lula," Abbi said, "even though she doesn't run away from anything. I remember what you said. It was dumb."

"It's smart. It's important. Run, and use anything in your power to make her run too."

"Oh," Abbi said. "That's different. Anything?"

"Anything, as long as it won't harm her."

"That's different." She nodded. "I'll try. I can try. I won't hurt her."

"Good," I said. "Thank you, pumpkin."

She grinned at the name.

I stepped up to the back door and tried the handle. It turned easily in my hand. Mad Mat either wasn't afraid of being disturbed or was expecting us.

"Come in, come in," Mad Mat's voice said from further in the house, as if he were putting on a dinner for friends. "You are exactly who I want to see. We've missed you."

Lorde was already moving, sniffing the air to catch a

scent of Lu. I followed right behind her, Abbi behind me.

The first room was a mud room, no washing machine or clothes dryer, just a utility sink.

Everything was white, the walls, ceiling, floor, including the sink, and shelves. *Landlady white.* The term filtered through my brain, and right behind it: *Why would a god need a rental?*

Lorde slipped out of the mudroom and into the kitchen. She scented the air, then headed down a dark hallway to the right. I turned that way, but Abbi scampered off across the kitchen opposite, scooting around the wall and into the next room in a flash.

Damn it.

The shadows around Lorde and me hadn't changed, even though Abbi was out of eyesight. Her power was strong enough to span the distance.

"You're late, in fact," Mad Mat continued. "I expected you to return much more quickly. Especially for this event. Have I overestimated you? Come closer and let me clear the air."

I thought Mad Mat was talking to me. But now I wasn't as sure. His voice projected the way people spoke when they were on their phone's speaker. As if talking louder would make the words clearer.

The walls were white, but the hallway dark, drenched in shadows. A row of picture nails peppered one wall, dull metallic sparks the only relief. The hallway ended at a closed door.

To the left, a threshold opened into the next room.

Dim yellow light flickered in that space. I stopped, still in shadow.

I signaled Lorde to stay down. A flick of her ear told me she understood. I pressed my back against the wall and leaned just enough to see into the room.

It was a smaller space than I had expected, which might serve as a living room. There was no furniture except a small Franklin stove in the corner, its black stove pipe jutting up to plunge into the wall.

The worn wall-to-wall carpet had been ripped back and rolled into a messy spiral, smashed against the vertical blinds, which canted sideways, slicing the darkness beyond the glass.

The exposed wooden floor was covered in symbols that pulsed and smoked and burned, magic twisted and bound in a way that made my headache spike and my throat seize.

There were ways to use magic, some healing and benign, others darker and violent.

This was a destruction of magic I'd never seen before, a chaos—

—*a century ago, claws striking from the dark, fangs tearing, Lula's scream*—

—a violence that broke the laws of nature and forced reality to succumb—

—*lying on the floor as monsters tore me apart, as Lula convulsed*—

—a magic nested deep in a hundred years of my nightmares.

This wasn't magic. It was power—god power—frayed and tortured, harnessed and wielded by a god.

The same stench of power that had fueled the monsters who attacked us all those years ago.

Coming face-to-face with that power sent my mind reeling, panic rising.

"Brogan," Mad Mat said from behind a curtain of shifting, burning magic. "No need to hide in the rabbit's shadow. I see you. You may be late, but you are just in time to see Lula breathe her last breath."

CHAPTER TWELVE

I stepped out of the hallway and into the room, Lorde growling beside me. As I crossed the threshold, a hissing, fizzing sensation rolled over my skin. Shadow stripped away, the room instantly brighter.

Mad Mat's eyebrows climbed. "I see I misjudged you." The smile was sickly and cruel. "You should be dead, my friend. Tethered spirit."

Mad Mat's hands were behind his back. A wall of power separated us, symbols flaring to life at the ceiling then falling to create a pile of ashes on the floor, chalking a line across the entire room.

Everything behind him was more difficult to see, as if a wall of water separated one reality from another.

Magic shifted like a hand over the water's surface.

Lula knelt in the corner to the left. Her hands were tied behind her back with a rope that was a snake, smoke, fire, steel, pulsing and shifting between forms in a rolling undulation.

Her head hung, the red of her hair blurred and

dulled by the wall of power between us. She wore a tank top and jeans, her bare feet curled beneath her. Magic glyphs pulsed and burned on her exposed skin, sending up thin tendrils of smoke.

I cataloged every detail in a second. Mad Mat hadn't moved. "How are you back in flesh?" The words were mildly curious. Nothing important, just a passing interest.

Which was false. Everything about Mad Mat was false, an illusion. This house was an illusion. That friendly voice was an illusion.

But the concentrated god power here was not an illusion.

"Gods watch me," I said. "And they seem to have an opinion on how alive or dead I might be. Let Lula go, and you and I will settle this."

Something in the room thumped, then went silent. I worried Abbi had made the sound trying to help.

Lorde took a step toward Lula.

"No." Mat pointed at the dog. She froze mid-step, whining.

The thump rose and fell again.

"Gods watch you?" Mad Mat sneered. "Do you mean Cupid? If he interfered with your death, he has done you no favors. Connections and destruction are nothing when the Grim Reaper has been denied his prey."

"Let Lula go," I repeated.

"Oh, I intend to. But not until I get what I am owed."

"I don't have the book."

"Of course you don't." Mad Mat drew one hand forward, flicking a finger. The book appeared floating in mid-air in front of him. "I have the gods' spell book. The Hunter brought it to me. What I want is the key."

I held very still. Lu had stolen the key, a slice of silver shaped like a crow's wing. She wore it on the chain around her neck, along with the stopwatch that could halt time and bridge the veil between the living and tethered spirits.

I wanted to look over and see if she still had the chain around her neck, but I kept my eyes on the god, afraid to tip my hand. "I don't have the key."

Mad Mat smiled, and it made my gut clench. Every instinct in my body kicked into fight or flight, but flight was winning.

I thought I heard the thump again through the ringing in my ears.

I inhaled and exhaled, forcing my feet to stay still, and forcing my gaze not to falter under the horror of the god's delight.

"You do have the key," the god said, "or rather, you could. You *will*. Once you are spirit again." Mad Mat's head tipped to one side, and his mask slipped. Beneath the image of Mad Mat was a visage of horror.

Sandpaper eyes, a woman's mouth stretched over ragged teeth, her laughter brutal. I had seen her in the car crash. I had seen her in the storage fire. "Your bones will be my key."

Her head snapped up, and the Mad Mat mask was back, the smile uncomfortably human.

"You see me now, too, don't you? I know you are the

key, because I made you the key, not the silver wing Lula hides. You and Lula are lock and key. Your souls, so tortured, so strange." Mad Mat licked his lips.

"All the years neither fully alive, nor completely dead. All the years she carried a shred of your soul in her heart and you carried a shred of hers. Do you know how rare that is?

"Do you know how difficult it is to find? Two souls who could endure? Whose *love*," the god chuckled through Mad Mat's mouth, "was strong enough to torture them, to force them to cling, hopelessly, to each other even though there was no promise of relief? Death never came for you, and yet you wouldn't let go."

Mad Mat flicked a finger. The book spun slowly, repositioning itself so that the front faced me.

The book was slim and tawny brown, worked with gold threads and bits of stone and metal. Its clasp had been carved in the shape of a bird in full dive, a loop of leather clutched in its talons.

The page edges were a deep red. For something so powerful, it looked like any other book.

Power, gods, people, books, were not always what they appeared to be.

"You were my greatest discovery. After years of scouring the universe looking for the spell book, I found you and Lula. Without you, this," a gesture made the book bob like it was floating in water, "could never be mine."

"Let Lula go," I said again. "And I'll do what you want."

The god squared Mat's shoulders, one hand still

behind his back, the smile evaporating faster than dew in the desert. "Lula is mine now. She has always been mine. When I'm done with you, when I've used you up, she will still be mine. You will no longer exist. Alive or dead. No one will care that you've been crushed to dust."

A flutter of movement shifted at the edge of my vision. Something small and quick in the darkened doorway to the left slipped into the room. It dashed along the baseboards, moving toward the line of ash in front of Lula.

Abbi's rabbit form was smaller than I'd ever seen her before, barely larger than a mouse. I didn't know if she could cross the ashes and find a way through the watery wall of magic to Lula, but I was going to give her every second to try.

"A lot of gods have promised me death." I strode toward Mad Mat and the god who puppeted him, my hands loose at my side. "None of them have made it stick. I hated you from the day you came sniffing around Lula at our bakery. You were worthless then, and you're worthless now. You've tried to kill me and failed. So shut the hell up."

Abbi pushed through the ashes and wriggled her way under the wall of watery magic. She hopped behind Lula.

To untie her.

To break the magic that bound her.

To save her and run, run, run.

All she needed was time.

"You want to use me up?" I said. "Do it." I stopped

just out of arm's reach, though a god didn't need to lay hands on me to do damage. "If I'm the key, then use me. I'm calling your bluff."

The thump was faint. It wasn't coming from the corner where Abbi was trying to save Lula.

Greed and dark delight tightened those cardboard eyes. "You are not immortal, Brogan Gauge. Your usefulness will not last forever. Put your hands on the book."

Abbi hadn't gotten Lu untied, and Lu hadn't noticed the little rabbit behind her. Lu hadn't moved since I'd stepped into the room.

I tracked her from the corner of my eye. Abbi hopped around to the front of Lula. Then she jumped *through* her. As if she were a projection. An illusion.

Lula didn't flinch.

Abbi repeated the process two more times, then squeezed back under the wall of magic and crossed over the ash.

Lula still hadn't moved, because that wasn't Lula. That was an illusion. Lula was trapped, here, but somewhere else.

I knew she was close, could feel the anger of her soul. But she was not behind that magic wall, not in that magic cage.

That was what Mad Mat wanted me to think.

Lorde was still mostly frozen. She managed to scratch at the floorboards, whining softly.

The thump rang out again, a boot hitting the floor from beneath the boards.

Lorde dug again.

The horror was swift. Mat had buried Lula under the house.

If I put my hand on the book, it would knock me out, exactly as it had two other times. I would not be able to save Lula.

"I haven't failed to kill you," Mad Mat said. "I haven't wanted you dead yet. But today, Brogan Gauge, is your lucky day." He flicked a finger again, and the book hovered closer to me.

Mad Mat hadn't touched the book once. Even back at the Junk Hunt—there had been a glow of power protecting his hand.

"You can't touch it," I said. "The book chooses who owns it, who can touch it, who can use it. It doesn't want you."

The god scowled. "I am not such a fool as to leave my mark on this book. Not until it's open. Not until it's unlocked. Then. Then I will rip out each page and devour every spell. Their power will be my power."

My left hand lifted without my permission, my skin frozen and burning as if it were covered in ice and fire.

"If I wanted to touch it," Mad Mat said, using my hand like it was his own, "I would."

My breath hissed through locked teeth, as I breathed through the pain.

"But you, you are so much more convenient." Mad Mat's left hand drew forward from behind his back. "This, so much more satisfying."

A beautiful brass mouthpiece, the one that had looked so out of place on the trombone, shone in his hand.

Eunice's stolen reed. I heard the song and magic of it now that it was not attached to the trombone, soft and low as an owl's croon, the roll of a distant drum, the bass echo of universes brushing against each other as they spun across the void.

"Goodbye, for the last time, Brogan Gauge."

My hand stretched, fingers straightening toward the book.

Lorde dug furiously at the hard floor, and the little rabbit darted out of the room.

Good, I thought. *At least Abbi ran. At least she'll be safe.*

The thumping continued, harder now, Lula slamming the boards with all her strength. Lorde barked and barked.

"Hey!" A small voice, but strong. A child's voice, but ancient. The rabbit. The moon.

No, I thought, tried to yell, my voice clogged with pain. *Run!*

But Abbi did not run. She stood, a luminous blue-white light surrounding her, ink-black shadow at her back.

"I see you, Atë, I can *see* you in him," she said. "Your magic is frayed and weak. Easy to break. So I'm going to break it." She lifted her fist and threw something small and rectangular at the god.

It was a tin-coated box, the harmonica, flashing copper, pewter, gold, through the air. That's what she'd run for. She'd retrieved the harmonica from the duffle.

That wasn't all she'd retrieved. She gripped her mortar and pestle, grinding the magic that lapped the edge of the bowl, speaking in the language of power that lifted to her command.

The harmonica wailed as if a great wind pumped through it, and transformed into barn owls, dozens of them, moon faces screeching and hissing, talons extended. They dove at the god's face.

"Enough!" The power in the god's voice stopped the owls mid-flight and reduced them to ribbons of smoke and moonlight.

"No!" I yelled.

The power hit Abbi hard enough, she slammed into the wall behind her.

It was a second, less than that, but the god's grip on my hand loosened.

Beneath my cuff, the letter opener slipped, the sharp edge hot, pushing against the thin skin over my vein like a lick of flame, a promise. Gold. My vision flared with gold.

The same gold that had filled the place where I met Death.

The same gold that sparkled in Lula's eyes.

The same gold as the letter opener that was much, much more than a letter opener.

It was magic. It was power. It was changed by Death. And it was mine.

I shifted my wrist and the edge of the blade nicked my skin.

It was just a scratch. No deeper than a paper cut.

Just enough to let the magic know me, as it had known Death.

Gold, silver, copper, and black filled my mind, my

nostrils, my mouth. Rich, slick, hot magic poured into me.

My hand had stalled above the book. I could feel the power radiating from it, drawing me in.

It would be easy to grab the book. Use that power against the god.

But Eunice had told me to choose the reed over the book. She'd said it was important. Vital I do so. I had no damn idea how to get the reed away from Mad Mat.

Abbi struggled up to her feet. "I called him!" she shouted, one fist on her hip, the other thrust straight out, a tiny silver dime pinched in her fingers. "He's coming for you."

Mat turned his full attention to her. "You threaten me?" he hissed. "Run, rabbit." The Mat mask twisted into a horror of teeth and tentacles and eyes. "Run." He took a step her way.

I slipped the dagger into my palm and lunged.

In one swift movement, I plunged the weapon into his neck.

Mad Mat screamed, spinning to strike me, his other hand clawing at the dagger. I ducked the god's hit, shoved in closer, wrestling the mouthpiece out of his hand. But he was strong. Much stronger than me.

My grip on the mouthpiece slipped.

The room rocked, earthquake rattling the heavens, the earth heaving in great sideways jerks and drops. The god reeled backward, and I wrested the reed away.

Walls crumbled, wood and brick and mortar pouring down. Magic crashed and screeched into a sea of sound below us, above us, everywhere, deafening.

The house was coming down. Everything was coming down.

Lula was under the floor. I had to free her before we were buried alive. I stumbled backward, losing my feet.

Darkness swallowed the room, then cleared just enough I saw Abbi crouching next to Lorde. "He's coming! He's coming. Faster, Brogan. We have to dig faster!" She dug at the floorboards with Lorde, trying to pry them loose.

I pushed up to my knees, my head ringing. The blackness flashed with panther eyes—Hado's eyes—as he stood between us and the screaming god, hiding us in darkness.

The god might not see us, but I could see him. Mad Mat flickered in and out of focus, the dagger wedged deep in his throat. His face twisted, warped, and melted, teeth chewing through the illusion, tentacles lashing.

The face warped again, female and furious, blood-red lips chanting words that hammered like an avalanche.

I stowed the reed in my pocket and crawled to Abbi and Lorde. Lorde had been digging non-stop, her thick, strong claws tearing through the wood, leaving deep gouges. She'd dug hard enough, one of the boards was broken.

I eased her back from the space and grabbed the board's rough edges, prying upward.

The house was shaking apart. It took every bit of my strength to hold on to the board, and strength I didn't know I had to yank it free.

Then the clean crack of a storm breaking open filled

the air. I could smell rain, cool and fresh as lightning, that pierced the endless thunder.

This was magic. Different magic.

This was god power.

Cupid.

The floor dissolved into sand revealing Lula.

Blindfolded, gagged, hands tied behind her back, feet bound together, Lula kicked again, as she had been kicking this whole time. But there was no floor above her.

I dodged the strike and pressed my palm to her face.

"I've got you, I've got you, you're okay, we're okay." I was babbling, not caring what came out of my mouth, unable to hear my voice. I pushed the blindfold off her eyes and worked the gag down to her chin.

She breathed my name, her lips swollen and bleeding, her eyes blown from the sudden light. I needed to untie her hands, her boots, but time, as the seer had said, was not on our side.

I scooped Lula into my arms. Abbi was where the doorway had been, frantically motioning me forward. Lorde ran that way and I followed. Hado, now a giant, silent panther, ran beside me.

The god who had been Mad Mat was now molten fire, skin a roiling hellscape, volcanos for eyes. It clutched the book between its hands and roared.

A silver arrow sliced through its chest.

Cupid no longer looked like a biker. He was a towering, massive, powerful being with murder in his eyes and a deadly bow in his fist. Battle armor covered his chest and legs, inscribed with symbols that shifted and rewrote themselves, merging and snapping apart, generating and channeling his power. Huge wings, supernova bright, carved the sky above him.

He notched another arrow to his string and sent it singing through the god's head. The god that had been Mad Mat stumbled to its knees.

Cupid spared us a glance, notched another arrow, and shot it into the ground.

The earthquake rumbled and stalled out. But the sky, the air, the world itself streaked with hissing bolts of blackness, as if someone were pulling a thread and unraveling reality.

Cupid. God of connections and destruction. He could destroy any reality if he wanted.

This reality, this illusion made by the god who had been Mad Mat, was shredding apart.

The fiery god roared and rushed Cupid.

An explosion rocked the world.

Abbi grabbed my sleeve and pulled. I stumbled after her, the damned brace slowing me. She leaped ahead, quicker and more nimble than me, then came back, urging me to run fast, faster.

With Lula in my arms, I could only manage a slow jog, and even then, I was losing my breath, losing my strength. Wherever this reality was, I didn't think Lula and I were going to make it out.

"Run," I gasped. "Abbi, run."

She made a frustrated sound, then jumped and stared up into the sky.

"Oh," she said. "Owls."

The arc of the heavens was made of feathers, soft

and silent. The owls, hundreds, thousands, flew through the air, a wing, a wave of speed and hunt. Looking. They were looking for us.

The utter quiet of that many living creatures so close above us struck a familiar chord.

"Eunice," I croaked, no longer running. "I chose your reed. Over the book. I have it. I have your reed."

The wings swooped closer, hovering in the air and enveloping us, soft as a breath, a sigh.

What was left of the house behind us blasted apart. Feathers tucked in tighter, shielding us as the force from that explosion propelled us forward.

The song of glass beads, shells, and wooden charms mixed with the ringing in my ears.

And then, we fell.

CHAPTER THIRTEEN

Being alive came with aches and pain. The way I saw it, the physical pain of living was the easiest to endure.

For me, the pain of loss, of grief, of hopelessness—that was bigger, abstract. I had no tools to fight it, no hands to grapple with it. Grief drank all the air out of my lungs, leaving me gasping for the strength it took to swim to shore where those I loved were safe. Unharmed.

Lula, buried, gagged, and bound.

Abbi running.

The explosion.

All of it a wave of fear, of grief, cresting and dragging me down, squeezing life out of my bones, silencing the beat of my heart.

I gasped, and my ribs gave a good argument for not trying any other sudden moves. My eyes hurt, and I hadn't even opened them yet. Every inch of my skin felt burned.

Something soft brushed my lips, tentative and silken, like a feather, a moth's wing.

A kiss.

"Lula?" I asked, her name blown to smoke before it even left my lips.

"I'm here." Her voice like dawn, golden and soft. "Can you open your eyes?"

For her, anything. I had to work at it, though, my eyelids heavy and sticky. I blinked against the light, and after several tries, could make out shadows, light, shape, and then Lula.

She hovered above me, sitting on the side of the bed in a room I did not remember. A frown line creased her forehead, but her lips relaxed as if a smile was waiting in the wings.

"I love you," she said, as she always had.

"I love you," I said, as I always would.

She leaned down and kissed me again, too tentatively until I deepened it, lifting my hand to cup the back of her head.

When we pulled apart, her pupils were enormous, the honey of her eyes a solar flare around that darkness. "I thought," she said, and then a breath huffed out of her. She licked her lips, which were not swollen, not bleeding. "You are never allowed to die on me again, Brogan Gauge."

"Never," I agreed. "If... When we go, we go together."

"We're staying," she said, her gaze covering my face as if I would argue her point. "We're both staying for now."

"I intend to live a long life with you, wife," I said. "That's always been the plan."

She nodded, her eyes glittering with the promise of tears.

"I see you're awake," Eunice said from somewhere near my feet. Might be standing in the doorway, but I didn't care to look away from my love's face to find out.

"Come out for food," she said when I didn't answer. "You have a visitor."

A creak of hinges told me I'd guessed right about the door. Then a weight landed on the bed on the other side of me, and Lorde whined and pressed along my body, carefully wedging her big head between Lula and me. She licked Lula's chin, then plonked her head on my chest, panting up at me, the smell of dog breath over-powering.

"Ugh," Lula said. "You stink, Lorde."

Lorde flicked her soft, fuzzy ears and panted harder.

"We have company?" I asked.

"I don't know." Lula rubbed the dog's head. "I don't care. We could stay here."

There was hope in her voice and behind that a spider-silk thread of worry, vulnerability. I had all but died, and she had been bound and buried. We hadn't had time to deal with any of that. To know that we had survived, together.

"Are you hurt?" I ran my fingers over her hair, callouses catching in the soft waves. "Did the god hurt you?"

She shook her head, and I knew she was lying.

"Ah, Lula," I said softly.

She was still shaking her head. I pressed my palm against her cheek and she closed her eyes. A tear trickled down her cheek and warmed between my skin and hers.

"Tell me?" My anger was distant. I would deal with it later. Right now, all that mattered was Lula and what she needed from me.

"It wasn't…it wasn't physical. But the god…You died, Brogan. Mad Mat showed me…you died." The last word hitched. She tried to smile, but it broke as tears ran freely now. She swiped at her face, frustrated at the emotion.

"I didn't die though. No, wait. Listen, love." I tried to sit, but there was a lot of dog in my way. It took a minute to talk Lorde into moving to one side, then there were the ribs that made sitting and breathing an either/or thing, before I finally settled my back—carefully—against the headboard of the narrow bed.

"Let me get you something," Lula said, swallowing until her voice was steady. "Water?"

"Just you, love," I said, patting my chest in invitation. "Come here. The world can spin without us for a minute or two."

She shook her head again, but it was a tiny thing. She eased back down onto the bed and carefully—much too carefully—rested her head against my shoulder, her hand over my heart, her knees tucked up against my hip.

I waited until my breathing was even, waited until some of the strain in her muscles relaxed.

"I didn't die," I whispered, my hand spread across her back, holding her to me.

She made a noise, and I went on. "No, love. I really didn't. I met Death, but I didn't die."

She leaned away to look back at me. "You met Death. The god of death?"

"Yes."

"Are you sure? He might have been another god. A trickster. A liar. An illusion, like Mat."

"No, it was Death. He was…not what I expected. He said he's on vacation. He had a shirt with Ordinary, Oregon, on it."

"The vacation town for gods is named Ordinary? Really?"

I tipped my head. "Maybe."

"What was he like? What did he say?"

"Intense, and not unkind. I would almost say he was funny, but amused might be a better word. He radiated power, just…everywhere. He told me he wasn't home, so he wouldn't let me into the house of death, and basically didn't agree with my dying."

"He can do that?"

"He said he's older than a lot of gods and can bend the rules."

"That's…not comforting."

"He said the god who was using Mad Mat has been hunting us for years. Us and the book, and that that god was the one who sent the monsters to…to change us, bind us to the road."

Her face and settled into the sharp lines of anger.

No, not anger. Determination.

"So we're killing a god?" Steady as a mountain, my wife. Cold as steel.

"Looks like it. Have to find the god first."

"And the book," she said.

"Not sure I want the book to be involved."

"You know why Mad Mat wanted you dead? You know why he buried me?"

"He—Mad Mat isn't a man. He's…she's a god named Atë. Mad Mat is just an illusion, a shape she's using. Atë wants the spell book of the gods and thinks we can open it for her. Death said… I think he thinks we can use it."

"But not alive?" she asked. "Atë sent the monsters to bind us to the road and tried to kill you after Cupid had brought you back. Atë wants you a tethered spirit, Brogan, and me a monster."

"Hey, now." I didn't argue, because she was right. Still, I rubbed her back again. We were quiet for a moment.

"If Atë is a god," Lula said, "Why can't she use the spells in the book on her own?"

"Because," a deep voice said from the doorway, "she wasn't one of the gods who offered a spell for the book."

Cupid was in his biker form again. Bald head, white beard, jewels in his ears. Tattoos of the dove on one hand and owl on the other and more tattoos twining up his arms. Biker-black leather vest over a black T-shirt, jeans, and boots—also black—finished the look.

"Eunice has tea and food, if you'd like to join us," he said.

Lorde hopped off the bed and trotted over to him like she'd forgotten we existed. She wagged her tail and *woof*ed softly.

Cupid knelt in front of her and rubbed at her ears. "Hello there, girl," he said. "Have you been keeping an eye on them for me?"

She made a growly, vocal sound.

"Yes, you are a good girl. Finding Lula. Very good girl." There was a bone in his hand now, and he offered it to her.

Lorde took it delicately from his fingers, her tail still wagging. He gave her side a pat, a soft smile on his face, then flicked a glance our way. "I'll see you in the kitchen when you're ready." He walked out with Lorde following, absolutely smitten with him.

We waited until the sound of his boots on the wooden floor faded. He could probably hear us no matter how quietly we talked, but still, the illusion of privacy was nice.

"We could end our contract," I said. "Tell Cupid we're done looking for the book for him. We technically found it. Atë has it. We can tell him we're done running his errands."

Lula slid her hand in mine. "Do you really want him against us?"

"I'm not sure that's the position he'd take. He could just find two other unlucky clods to track down the book."

"Maybe Cupid already has the book. That fight with Atë. He might have taken it from her back at the house."

I inhaled as deeply as I could, ribs twinging, then blew the breath out. "I suppose we'll find out. Cup of tea with a god?"

"Coffee," she said. "Eunice has a special blend." She tugged on my hand, helping me swing my legs over the edge of the bed.

"How long have we been here?" I asked, unable to tell if it was day or night in the windowless room. I took a few shuffling steps and realized I needed to piss.

"Three days."

I scowled, unhappy at being unconscious for so long. "Three?"

She ducked under my arm and propelled me toward the door. "We've been fine. Eunice has been nice. Abbi's happy." That, she said a little quieter, and I knew why.

We were both growing fond of the little moon rabbit. But she had a bit of the wild in her. She had a way of making friends, making family, and then running off. She'd already joined and left behind two clans of werewolves who adored her.

"She called Cupid," I said, "after she figured out the illusion wasn't you."

"She told me. Often. A lot." Lu rolled her eyes. We'd stopped, and she opened the bathroom door. "I'll be in the kitchen." She pointed down the hall, lifted up on her toes, and kissed my mouth. "I love you."

Then she swayed down the hall, my everything, my today, my forever.

"Your truck's up and running," Eunice said as she handed me a mug of coffee. Lula was right—her coffee was delicious. "Lawrence Hobbs got a hold of me this morning. Said the mechanic's done with it, and even threw in some body work and paint. It's solid for the road again."

I wrapped my hands around the mug, enjoying the heat. I'd already downed one cup, several fluffy biscuits covered in butter and peach jam, and a plate of ham and potato hash with enough pepper to make my tongue sting.

Lu sipped her coffee at the table to my right, Abbi perched on a bench window seat where she could peer out the window at the Oklahoma morning. Hado was back in his tiny kitten form, curled in Abbi's lap.

Cupid sat across the table from Lu and I. He'd draped his leather jacket across his chair and was giving occasional attention to the mug that gave off the scent of hot apple cider and cinnamon.

"Thank you," Lula said. "We'll pick it up."

Eunice stood at where I thought was her power position in the room, leaning her hip against the sink. She crossed her arms over her chest, beads whispering. "Come on now," she said. "No use brooding. Let's talk this out."

"Don't know that there's anything to say," I said.

"Not you." She tipped her chin. "Cupid. You need to say your piece or all the gears of possibilities are gonna rust up."

"I agree with Brogan," he said. "There isn't much to say."

"No," she said. "That's not at all the truth. It's not even *your* truth. Say it out, Bo. Talk to these young souls. They just might be what you're hoping for."

"Ooooo," Abbi said, "is this an omen? A fortune

telling? How long is my lifeline? No, wait. Do I have a lifeline?" She held both hands toward Eunice, but Hado mewled a complaint, so she dropped them and went back to petting him.

Cupid scowled at his mug, then picked at the tabletop and brushed away an imaginary crumb.

"This is your moment, Old One." Voices behind her voice layered a song, a chant, a power as inexhaustible as the heartbeat of the universe. "This is your chance to shift the stars. Even Fate cannot stand in your way."

Cupid turned his scowl on her, then decided something, his shoulders rolling back. He ran his hand with the owl tattoo over the top of his head, fingers pinching the jewels in his ear before coming to rest on the table.

"If you want," he said, addressing Lu and me, words measured, "I will release you from your contract with me. Before you ask, I will not return you to spirit, Brogan. If you want, I will simply dissolve from you the burden of finding the spell book and of doing any of my bidding."

Lula held her breath, studying him, trying to see things not visible to the human eye. I grunted and set my mug down.

"Why?" I asked. "Why now?"

"I didn't expect Atë to be involved. I should have."

"Who is she?" I asked, which sounded strange. "I mean, what power does she have?"

"She is the god of ruin, mischief, blind folly. She has been banned from many realms of the gods and seeks revenge upon those who ostracized her. She has hunted the book for centuries. What better way to sow her chaos among the gods than with their own spells?"

He drummed his fingers on the table. Lorde moved closer and plunked her head on his lap. He scratched behind her ears and her tail thumped the floor.

"Illusion is one of her favorite tricks," he said. "That, and leading the gods to destruction. In finding the book, she now has a weapon. Deadly in her hands. This is not what either of you signed up for."

So Cupid hadn't been able to take it from her back at the house. I wondered how she'd gotten away from him. If she was injured.

"Finding the book is what we agreed to," I said.

"You found it," he said. "That fulfills your contract."

"We were supposed to return it to you."

"Not anymore. Lula and Brogan, I free you."

"We don't accept that," I said.

Abbi burped a little laugh, then cleared her throat to try to cover it.

"I have only your welfare in mind," Cupid said. "Don't be difficult."

I couldn't tell if he was annoyed or amused, but since he hadn't turned into a massive, winged warrior, I assumed he was willing to listen.

"You didn't kill her," I stated.

He shook his head.

"Did you wound her?"

"Yes."

"So she may not keep the book with her, fearing it could be tracked by you. By us, or others. Now might be the best chance to find the book, find where she may have hidden it."

"Or the worst," he countered.

"I think it's time to renegotiate," I said. Lu's hand under the table rested on my thigh. I laced our fingers.

"We have a stake in our own welfare. We have free will," I said. "Finding the book, getting it out of Atë's hands is important to us. We want to find the monsters that took our lives, even if that monster is a god."

"You don't want to declare war on Atë or any god," Cupid said. "If nothing else, trust my word on that."

"I didn't say we wanted war."

Did I want to see Atë bleed? Yes. But I was under no misconception that we could enter a fight with her and survive. There were other ways to kill a god, other weapons at our disposal.

"Atë wouldn't touch the book," I said. "There's a reason she wanted it in my hands. There's a reason she bound and gagged Lula and waited for me to come for her. She has plans for us."

Cupid sat back, his exhale loud. "Yes," he admitted. "She does."

"Death said Atë wanted me to remain a tethered spirit."

"Than? When did Thanatos speak to you?"

"When I touched the book, and it mostly killed me."

Cupid was silent, weighing that. "Mostly?"

"Death said my dying didn't agree with him, so he sent me back to life."

Cupid smiled, the first time since we'd come into the

kitchen. His eyes glinted. "Old man can't resist tipping Fate's scale. He's supposed to be on vacation."

"He said he's the sort of god who can bend rules."

Cupid chuckled. "Aren't we all?"

Eunice cleared her throat. "Death is *old*, Bo."

"As am I. All right," he said, "we renegotiate. Tell me what you want and what you offer."

"We want your help finding the book again," I said.

Lula squeezed my fingers so hard, I was losing feeling in them. "And when we find it, we want you to help us kill Atë."

Lightning flashed in his eyes, and Lorde whined softly. He patted her head gently, but the storm did not fade.

I waited. It was part of what we wanted, part of what we planned to do with him or without him, but it was not everything. We had learned not to trust gods. Not even this one.

"What are you offering me?" His voice was deceptively soft, and I knew I was treading a cliff edge with him.

He was the god of connection.

He was the god of destruction.

I hoped that would work for us and not against us.

"Our trust."

Lula's hand went slack, then she held on again. She leaned forward so she could speak to him around me.

"If this book could have been found by you, you would have found it," she said. "If this book could have been used by Atë, she would have used it. Both of you have come to us. Both of you have wanted to use us as tools to get to the book. Maybe for different reasons, maybe for the same.

"If you help us find the book, help us kill the god who has put us through years of hell, then we'll help you. We'll put our trust and our loyalty in you. Whatever power we have with the book, or *over* the book, we will use it for you."

It shouldn't be enough to catch a god's interest. We were just two people among billions. There had to be other people who could do what we did, who could find the book, unlock the book—

—use the spells within the book—

—contain the book's power. Whatever it was that tied us to this spell book, to the gods, had to be replicated in some other people in all the world. What chance did we have of making deals with forces much, much stronger than us?

"There are other mortals in this world," he said.

"No two like us." Lula called his bluff.

Eunice hummed, and it sounded like agreement.

Cupid stared off in the distance, searching horizons I could not see.

"You were born for this," he said, "more's the pity you had no say over it. I found you because I was curious. You were an anomaly. I didn't know a god was behind your pain, that she tore you apart, spirit and flesh. Once I found you, it was clear you were connected to the book. But how you are connected to it isn't something I'm familiar with." He smiled, and it was rueful.

"There are very, very few connections I don't understand, but how the spell book of the gods is tied to you is one. It isn't chance. It isn't because you have lived your lives bound to the Route, broken by Atë.

"There is something else about you, Lula and Brogan, that will forever draw you toward the collected powers of the gods."

"Neat," Abbi said, and then after a look from me, "Oh. Not neat. But you're going to look after them, right? You're still going to be a good god?"

"That's what we're trying to decide, little rabbit."

"Then I want to say some things too. I want to stay. With them."

Cupid shifted his gaze to her. "You think I would tear you away from them?"

"You do those things. Sometimes," she said.

"Is there a reason I should do that? To you? To them?"

"You might be mad. Sometime, when you know more things, you might be angry."

"What things?"

"No," Eunice said, her voice a clear note that cut through the kitchen and seemed to roll to the world's end. "That is not a question you should answer, Moon Rabbit. Not…not if the future is to tilt toward good."

"She has free will," Cupid grumped.

I huffed a laugh. "She does. She can ignore both of you if she wants."

"Okay," Abbi said. "This is my free will. I want to stay with Lula and Brogan. And I want you to keep being a good god."

Cupid made a noise in the back of his throat. "That's not exactly how free will works."

"Good god. You can do it. I've seen you, Cupid. Many years." And there was more behind her words than a young girl could deliver.

She was a deity, a power of her own, and had spent centuries on the moon, looking down on the earth. "I see you searching for more than just the book. You are searching for meaning. For why you should still exist. Why you should still carry that power. I've seen your fatigue. I've seen your restlessness.

"I've seen your goodness. That's what will matter. That's what will make this world tilt toward good."

"Who said I want the world to tilt toward good?" Cupid asked.

Abbi dropped her head to one side and closed one eye. "I *see* you, god."

"Then you know better than to ask me to bind you to Brogan and Lula. Did I not send them to find you? Or have you forgotten?"

"I just… Yes, I remember that. But I thought…" Her eyes cut to us, away, then back to us, and away again. "I thought you could make it stick."

"They have free will too, little rabbit," he said. "Perhaps you should ask them what they want."

Abbi looked down at Hado and nodded. "Still. You should be good. There aren't a lot of good gods."

"Time to wrap this up," Eunice said. "Make the decisions."

"You help us kill Atë," I said, "and we'll stay loyal. We'll help you. We'll help you with the book."

Cupid rubbed his thumb on the side of his mug, the motion ticking, ticking. Power gathered and thickened, bringing a sub-audible hum into the air like distant bees moving closer, heavy with pollen.

"What you're asking…" His thumb stopped. "It isn't easy to kill a god. Not one like Atë. But I would rather walk this road with you than have you stumble into something that will crack the gears of the world.

"You'll find that book with or without me. You've already found it twice. This then: Give me your word you will stay loyal to me."

There was weight to his words, power. The bees landed, feet pricking over the pores of my skin.

"Give me your word you will not use the book without me."

He knew. Or at least, he suspected, that we could use the book. Use the spells of the gods.

"Do you think we are strong enough to use the book? To cast a god's spell?" Lula asked.

"I think you've been strong enough not to die several times. I think you've been strong enough to touch the book twice and survive.

"All good things and bad things come in threes. When you find the book again, I want you to give it to me."

"What are you going to do with it?" The question was out of my mouth before I thought better of it, but it surprised him.

The power stilled, quivered.

"I will make sure it is lost and never found again."

"You'll destroy it?"

He exhaled slowly, and there was something very dangerous in his gaze. "No god can destroy it. Not even me. That, then, is a truth you now know, one we have not revealed to anyone. Brogan and Lula Gauge, I will have your promise. You will stay loyal to me."

"Yes," Lula said. "If you help us kill Atë, we will stay loyal to you."

She had guts, my wife. Steel resolve to bargain with a god and not give ground.

"Yes," I agreed simply.

"I give you my word and bond," Cupid said. "If I can kill Atë, I will do so."

The air compressed, hard and hot, a sun lowering to earth. The bees buzzed, loud and louder, a harmony, a war cry shouted by a thousand wings.

"I'll help you find the book," he said, setting this connection as only he could. The bees were flying now, wings moving the air, the world, calling in cooler winds, clearer skies.

"I'll see that it never falls into the wrong hands again. In return, you give me your loyalty, your word. You will not cross my will, my intent. You alone will not end this contract. Instead, we will exit it upon mutual agreement."

That was the hard part to swallow. Before, I had insisted that Lula and I could end this connection any time we wanted to. If we did this now, if we agreed to his terms, we wouldn't be free of the god unless he agreed to dissolve the connection.

"Agreed," Lula said.

How could I not follow where she led? I shook my head once, my shoulders dropping. "Agreed."

The first agreement we had made with Cupid had

felt like a blessing. Gentle in its hold, quiet as a sunrise. This connection was more. It was a solid thing made of lead arrows and gold bowstrings. It flexed, the tension promising flight, speed, and recoil.

We would not end this connection to the god quickly. We would not escape his hold easily.

"This then, our seal." Cupid's words eased the draw, slackened the string, leaving a soothing warmth behind.

"Oh," Abbi said. She stood next to Cupid—I hadn't even seen her move—Hado resting across her shoulders, staring up at the god intently.

He dropped his gaze to her.

She tugged his hand, and he bent slightly her way. "Thank you," she whispered in his ear.

"For what, little rabbit?"

"For them." She planted a quick kiss on his cheek, then trotted over to stand next to me. "I like this," she said. "I like it *so* far."

I wasn't sure I could agree with her, but the ache and pain I'd been carrying since I'd almost died had lifted away, making me lazy and relaxed. I hadn't felt this good since I'd come back into flesh.

Lula let out a breath she'd been holding and squeezed my hand gently. I ran my thumb across the soft skin of her knuckles. She shivered and sat back against the chair.

"Good." Eunice pushed off the counter's edge. "Now that you're all family, I think it's time to have cake."

"Family?" I asked. "We're not—"

Lula squeezed my fingers, just as Abbi took my other

hand. "A little right?" Her eyes were wide, hopeful. "A little like a family, because we have a reason to stay together. A reason to choose us together and look after each other."

"It's not—" I started again.

"You're right, Abbi," Lula said. "It's a little like a family."

"Brogan?" Abbi asked. "Like a family?"

Lorde padded around the table to Abbi, her mouth open in her doggy smile, her tail wagging. Abbi rested her hand on the dog's fuzzy shoulders.

I looked between all of them, the Moon Rabbit and her shadow, the happy black dog, the god who was watching all this with a curiously satisfied smile, the Muse, who was hauling the largest chocolate cake I'd seen in my life out of the refrigerator, and finally, my wife.

It was there that I stopped, in her, where I would always find my home.

She smiled, and it was the sunlight that eased my soul, the starlight by which my spirit navigated.

"Family?" I said, a question, a statement.

"Family," she agreed, a promise, a hope.

"Yes," I said to Abbi, though I couldn't look away from Lula. "Like a family."

CHAPTER FOURTEEN

The thing about sleeping in the back of an old truck under the Oklahoma sky was how the truck bed exactly fitted the five of us.

Lorde stretched across the back of the bed, her legs kicked out on the open tailgate, snoring away. Abbi curled into our brave, fuzzy dog, her arm across Lorde's ribs. Tiny kitten Hado was curled up on Lorde's neck.

Abbi breathed deeply and evenly, lost to whatever dreamland a Moon Rabbit dreamed.

I sat against the back of the cab, my legs stretched out, a pillow keeping the edge of the bed from digging in too hard.

Lula sat next to me, her head on my shoulder, face tipped to the stars, my arm relaxed around her and holding her close.

The wind smelled of weeds and bark and summer gone sweet and dry, crickets and other critters making a soft, steady racket, filling out the emptiness of the night.

We'd pulled off a ways into a field, red oak and

black walnut trees keeping us mostly hidden from the worn path of Route 66.

"Cake was good," I said.

Lula nodded. I'd mentioned the cake half a dozen times since we'd left Eunice's place a day ago. Abbi had told Eunice it was the best cake she'd ever eaten in all her long life, and while that compliment had gotten her an extra slice, I didn't think she was lying.

"Eunice is good people," Lula said. "I think she wanted things to turn out this way."

"What? Us sleeping in the truck?"

"That, and other things. Us pledging loyalty to Cupid. Finding the book, discovering Mad Mat was Atë, and Atë was the one who sent the monsters after us."

She paused. Then, "Making a little family for Abbi."

I hummed and stroked the curve of her arm.

The wind stirred, soft as an eddy in a stream harbored away from the swift current.

"She wanted the reed," I said, "though she might have wanted to put her own spin on the future too."

"Maybe."

"Worth it, if we can get the book and end this."

Lula made a small sound of agreement. "Not all of it," she said after some time had slipped by, minutes like leaves on the slow-moving water.

"What?"

"You said end this. I don't want all of this to end." She tipped her face up, eyes full of starlit jewels.

"That so?" My heart beat strong and steady, like I'd hiked a day of hills and had settled down to rest my head on the soft grass.

"I want to keep doing this, here," she said, "with you real in my arms."

"Camping in an old truck in nowhere, Oklahoma?"

She squinted. "Holding on to each other," she groused. Then, softer, "Talking, building our life. Our family. I want a hell of a lot of living years with you, Brogan Gauge. After we find that book, after we kill that god."

"You'll have them," I said.

"That easy?"

"Always. There's nowhere for me but with you, Lula Gauge. Your road is my road, your dreams my dreams."

"And my nightmares?"

"Like I'd ever leave you to face them alone. You know me."

She lifted her hand and traced the edge of my jaw. "Can't hurt to know you a little more."

"Is that an invitation?" My heart slowed, but the beat was harder, thick with anticipation, desire.

"Yes. You are invited to help me clean up the mess of our storage unit. You are invited to help me deal with Headwaters not getting what he wanted. You are invited to help me try to keep Abbi out of every cookie aisle and candy stand from here to the Pacific."

"And?" I said, shifting, so that we slid down deeper into the heavy covers, the mattress we'd laid across the truck bed soft beneath us.

"And?" she asked, as I rolled so that I was propped on one arm and she was below me made of moonlight: liquid silver, supple, and beautiful.

"And I want our tomorrows," I said.

She swallowed, her eyes closed. When she opened them again, they glittered with tears. "I didn't think it would happen, not after…everything." She laughed, and it broke. "But it can. We can have that. Days together. Years. We aren't going to be cheated out of it again."

"No, we aren't." I wiped my thumb across her cheek, catching her tear. "But I'd say you might should slow down on making deals with gods that have no return policies."

"And you need to stop dying."

"Easy enough. I don't do that very well, anyway."

Her smile rose, fell. "We're going to kill that god," she said, and I nodded. "We're going to get that book," she said, and I nodded. "We're not going to give the book to Cupid, are we?"

I shook my head. "If he can't destroy it, we will."

We were quiet a moment, knowing there would be consequences to that choice. Possibly bad ones.

Finally, she nodded. "I love you, Brogan Gauge," she said, as she always had.

"I love you too, Lula Gauge," I replied, as I always would. "Let's get us a lifetime of tomorrows together."

She nodded, but just to be sure, we kissed to seal the deal.

Devon Monk is a USA Today bestselling fantasy author. Her series include Ordinary Magic, Souls of the Road, West Hell Magic, House Immortal, Allie Beckstrom, Broken Magic, and the Age of Steam steampunk series. Her short fiction can be found in various anthologies and in her collection: A Cup of Normal.

Devon lives in lovely, rainy Oregon. When not writing, she is drinking too much coffee, watching hockey, or knitting ridiculous things.

Want to read more from Devon?

Follow her blog: www.devonmonk.com sign up for her newsletter, or check out the social media below.

House Immortal

Infinity Bell

Crucible Zero

BROKEN MAGIC

Hell Bent

Stone Cold

Backlash

ALLIE BECKSTROM

Magic to the Bone

Magic in the Blood

Magic in the Shadows

Magic on the Storm

Magic at the Gate

Magic on the Hunt

Magic on the Line

Magic without Mercy

Magic for a Price

AGE OF STEAM

Dead Iron

Tin Swift

Cold Copper

Hang Fire (short story)

SHORT STORIES

A Cup of Normal (collection)

Yarrow, Sturdy and Bright (Once Upon a Curse anthology)

A Small Magic (Once Upon a Kiss anthology)

Little Flame (Once Upon a Ghost anthology)

Wish Upon a Straw (Once Upon a Wish anthology)